BOTS

CONTROL
ARCHITECTURE

Nicole M. Taylor

EPIC
Press

Control Architecture
Bots: Book #6

Written by Nicole M. Taylor

Copyright © 2016 by Abdo Consulting Group, Inc.

Published by EPIC Press™
PO Box 398166
Minneapolis, MN 55439

Cover design by Dorothy Toth
Images for cover art obtained from iStockPhoto.com
Edited by Jennifer Skogen

LIBRARY OF CONGRESS CATALOGING-IN-PUBLICATION DATA

Taylor, Nicole M.
Control architecture / Nicole M. Taylor.
p. cm. — (Bots ; #6)
Summary: The great Bot recall begins with General Liao demanding nothing less
than the total obliteration of all humanoid robots. Hart must make unexpected allies
in the corporate world or they both will face the same fate: annihilation.
ISBN 978-1-68076-006-4 (hardcover)
1. Robots—Fiction. 2. Robotics—Fiction. 3. Young adult fiction. I. Title.
[Fic]—dc23
2015932716

EPIC
Press

EPICPRESS.COM

"Control Architecture": *Def. The elaborate framework, both software and hardware, that controls any robotic system.*

ONE

TARGET ACQUIRED

THE USS WOODROW WILSON, NORTHERN PACIFIC. JUNE, 2047

The collective, the group, the hive, the resistance—Sheba thought of it in different terms—had no official hierarchy. Though some individuals specialized (as Sheba did in performing modifications), no one Bot could be said to be "above" another. Officially.

Unofficially, when Hart and her small team left the ship to go directly to Washington and engage with that idiot congressman who had gutted the Bot bill in a fit of pique, Sheba knew that she was in charge.

It didn't mean much, being in charge. At least, not when things were going well. The Bots on the ship knew their business and they certainly did not require oversight to get things done. Occasionally, one or two Bots would come to some sort of disagreement that they could not decide between themselves and then they might seek out Sheba and ask for her advice, ostensibly as if she were a disinterested observer. In reality, Sheba knew that the moment the helicopter carrying Hart had lifted off from the flight deck, her thoughts and words increased in value and weight.

It was rare, however, that she was required to mediate in the daily doings of the other Bots, many of whom, she suspected, had not even realized that Hart was gone. Thus her job, in Hart's absence, looked remarkably like her job as she normally performed it. For Sheba, this meant seeing to the humans.

Sheba had not wanted the humans. She argued strenuously against keeping any of them—even the most grievously wounded—aboard. "They can take care of their own," she had said. But Sheba had been overruled. Hart did not say, exactly, that the humans were hostages or bargaining chips but it was understood that the great mass of them—more than a thousand—represented a kind of small insurance policy. Would the Army kill a thousand of its own to crush the Bot resistance? Possibly, but the decision would not be easy and it would not be quick.

Sheba sometimes thought that all their decisions were simply about buying more time in ever-shrinking increments.

Now that the humans were aboard and there was nothing she could do about it, someone had to look after them. As de facto head of the human modification program, Sheba had settled into the role involuntarily, like water dribbling into the empty shape left by a glacier.

Hart had made it very clear to her that she was to offer modification but not force it upon anyone. That would have been one way of securing acceptance from the humans: convert enough of them into Bots, or something very like it. But Sheba could not imagine that any Bot would be comfortable doing that sort of thing. Nearly every Bot in existence knew from painful and intimate experience what it was to be shaped and changed and transformed without ever being asked.

Besides, Bot-modded humans were not, in Sheba's experienced opinion, anything approaching a real Bot in terms of utility and skill. The human body was made of profoundly weak materials, inferior versions of even the shoddiest Bot's infrastructure. Human-Bot modification was a one-way street as far as Sheba was concerned, and there was nothing in it to benefit Bots as a whole. In the future, she imagined that no self-respecting Bot would perform the procedures.

Most of the humans did not request mods. Some actively insisted against them and Sheba noted that in their files. There had been others, though, right after the carrier was taken, who were gravely wounded and unable to answer questions about their personal philosophical approach to Bot-human integration. Sheba had done her best by them. Many lived, a few died, some of them were not happy with the outcome.

She had done very few brain mods and minimal ones at that. Nothing that would cause major personality changes or create . . . uncomfortable complications. Nevertheless, some of the humans reacted as though she'd fastened a rat's tail to their arm or leg. They acted as though Bot tech—stronger than their damaged limbs, more durable, more flexible, superior in literally every way—was somehow dirty and would contaminate them. It was insulting, the way they looked at her as though she were some kind of butcher. As though she were one of *them*. She, who remembered every single modification, every cut, every stitch, every addition and every subtraction.

One patient in particular was a chore. A very young man who would, without Sheba's intervention, be minus one entire arm from the shoulder down. They had to move him far away from the rest of them because he wouldn't stop agitating the other humans, trying to get them to stage some sort of mutiny.

They kept him in what Sheba thought had once been a storage room. It was deep in the bowels of the carrier and sound did not carry far outside its thick metal walls. They also had to restrain him to his hospital bed, something Hart had wanted to avoid. But it was either the restraints or over the side. Sheba knew which one she would have picked, but no one had asked her.

She started her rounds every morning with the young man, Seaman Joshua Lersher. She stripped his dressing, which he should have stopped wearing nearly a week ago, and inspected the seam where the Bot-flesh joined his human body.

"Congratulations," she said, "it's infected again." She had no idea how he had managed to keep his incision from healing for so long, especially with his wrists secured to the bed rails. It was as though he could actually will his body to reject the Bot addition.

The boy didn't say anything to her—he rarely deigned to speak directly to the Bots—but she could see his delight all over his smug little face. They both knew what had to happen now: Sheba would need to give up on the arm and remove the replacement she had crafted so painstakingly for him.

"It'll go to someone else," she said, though she could not imagine why she bothered. He just lay there, smiling silently up at her as though she were the most hilarious joke he had ever heard. The arm *would* go to someone else, in one form or another and Sheba could be sure that other person would be more grateful, more deserving. At the very least, they would definitely be less of a pain in Sheba's ass.

"We don't have to keep you alive," she told him, though that wasn't really true. In the macro sense, of course, the Bots could simply stop feeding the humans, or stop running the onboard desalination plant that provided them with the fresh water that Bots did not require. That, however, was not Sheba's decision to make.

It was his grin, though, that bothered Sheba more than the unhealed incision. His grin looked . . . incorrect. It seemed as though the tight edges of his mouth sunk more deeply into his flesh than she remembered. It was as though his face were subtly puffier. Sheba reached forward and felt along the edges of his throat, down from his earlobes. He tossed his head, trying to shake off her fingers.

Sheba slapped him without intention. It was as though her hand had reached out of its own accord and connected soundly with his cheek like a magnet smacking against another. "Knock it off," she said, "it's for your own good."

Seaman Lersher was sullen but pliable as she palpated his lymph nodes only to discover that, sure enough, they were slightly swollen. It could have been his body's response to the infection in his arm but Sheba had doubts. She had started seeing a similar swelling in some of the other modded patients. It began in the lymph nodes but the swelling spread outwards, leaving the victims looking like hamsters with their cheeks packed full of seeds. There were three other such patients in the past two weeks, all of them modded humans and Sheba had been watching them closely to see if they developed other symptoms.

Sheba was not, for all her surgical skill, an actual doctor. Or rather, a doctor for humans. Nor did she have much on hand in the way of medical supplies. The ship had an infirmary but it was hardly equipped to handle an outbreak of . . . something? Sheba didn't even have a guess. With only the facial swelling to go on, it could have been any number of illnesses. Or it could have been something entirely new and different. After all, a modded human was unlike any other human who had gone before.

This would necessitate a change in protocol.

The first order of business would be to stop the spread of this . . . virus, perhaps? The second order of business would be to figure out exactly what it was. It was entirely possible that this was nothing more than a very strange symptom of rejection but, on the off chance that it wasn't . . . Hart would not want the carrier to become some sort of floating plague house.

"Well," Sheba said briskly, "looks like you might be getting some company."

Seaman Lersher wasn't smiling anymore now. He had watched her face carefully as she examined him and he apparently didn't like what he saw there. "What's wrong with me?" he asked. Was this the first time he had spoken to her directly?

"You've made yourself sick," Sheba said, though it was equally likely that Sheba herself had made him sick, or at least had been the most likely vector of disease. No sense in giving him that satisfaction. "You'll have to be quarantined."

"What's wrong with me?"

"I don't know," Sheba said tightly. "I do not treat humans."

"Then I want a human doctor."

"Well, if you've got one hiding in your pocket, let me know."

"You can't refuse me treatment. There are rules, treaties—"

Sheba laughed at him. "None of your rules apply to us." Seaman Lersher stared up at her with such perfect, undiluted hatred that Sheba could not help but be taken aback. She did not, however, let any of that show on her face. She wondered about the young man. He had worked here on the ship. Did he have Bot co-workers, Bot fellow sailors? What had he thought of them then, when they all shared the labor (the Bots, of course, taking the lion's share)?

"Relax," she told him firmly. "If we wanted to kill you, we would do it outright. You'll get better care than you deserve." Probably better care than he would have gotten in a stateside human hospital, for that matter. Sheba may not have known much about human diseases at the moment, but if she could get access to the global wifi, she could learn everything she needed to know.

But she had already spent more time than she could spare on this obstinate ass.

"We'll schedule a surgery," she said, taking out a roll of bandages and her little spool of medical tape, "and remove the arm. For now, please don't agitate it further. You may think this is some game or power play but it won't hurt me one little bit if you give yourself blood poisoning." She placed a clean gauze pad over the weeping incision and began to wind the bandages around shoulder joint and under his arm pit.

It was then that the floor beneath them shifted, jolted, nearly sent Sheba stumbling into the metal railing of Lersher's bed. For one moment, barely more than a few seconds, Sheba and Lersher were on the exact same page and, when they looked at one another, they saw the very same thing in each other's face.

Distantly, there was a deep groan with a high-pitched edge, like a wounded giant keening. And the boy in the bed started to smile. The smile turned into a laugh. It was surprisingly jolly, the laugh of a fat man, not a stick-thin boy.

"What the hell was that?" Sheba asked him. She could hear something else too, a silken sort of sound that was familiar, though she couldn't put a name to it.

"What, you don't know?" The boy was still laughing. "I thought you Bots knew everything."

Water, Sheba realized. That silken sound was moving water. A huge amount of moving water, somewhere close.

The boy reached out so fast that his plastic restraints thunked against the metal bed. He snatched Sheba's hand and held it in a violent grip. He found her eyes and smiled as he said: "That was a torpedo, bitch."

TWO

DEAD IN CALIFORNIA

NORTHERN CALIFORNIA, JUNE, 2047

Hart had not felt pain in a very long time. For her, pain served no purpose at all. If she were damaged and in need of repair, she could determine that from a simple visual or tactile assessment. Pain, or rather the diluted memory of it, did not help her evaluate and choose from a plethora of potential actions. Her ability to investigate and quantify the possible outcomes of a given action helped her make those choices. In fact, Hart had often discovered that it was the most painful actions that were the most necessary.

Her last experience with pain had been so long ago, in fact, that she almost didn't recognize what she was feeling when the little banner at the bottom of the cafe's television screen read: TERRORIST BOT DEVELOPER EDMOND WEST DEAD IN CALIFORNIA.

At first, she froze. She sat still and silent in front of a cup of coffee that she would not drink, across from a dour woman she could not acknowledge. Instead, her eyes were locked on the screen over the woman's shoulder, on the ticker at the bottom. She watched as it cycled through the news about elections in former Poland, desalination protests in Southern California, controversy over SennTech's newest line of hyper-realistic ChildBots, and then, finally, again, those same words.

Edmond. Dead.

In that moment, Hart realized that she had not really believed that Edmond went over the side of the aircraft carrier. If she had really believed that, if she had really grieved for him, she would not feel now as though someone had torn open a hole inside of her, all the way down to her bones.

Her mouth opened, to let out a cry that she could not generate. Instead, there was silence and blankness. Finally, the woman across from her—a liaison for a New York congresswoman—noticed her plight.

"Are . . . are you okay?"

But Hart was already standing up, letting her chair fall away behind her. She left her coffee, her coat, the purse she carried. All the things she used to pretend that she was human.

Hart did not look back.

———o———

The high-speed train went from Washington D.C. to San Francisco three times per day. Hart caught the last departure, sparsely populated with the usual contingent of suited professionals and students slouching under the weight of backpacks and messenger bags.

She used the seatback flex-tablet to sift through

news reports on Edmond. None seemed to have that much more information than the ticker scrawl had offered.

"Whoa," came a voice uncomfortably close to her shoulder. "They finally killed that guy, huh?"

Hart had chosen a seat in the back of the carriage and spread a convenient newsletter about the high speed rail over the accompanying seat in the hopes that she would not be forced to share. A young man in a pastel button-down ignored her unsubtle signal.

Hart spared him a single glance and gleaned everything she needed to know from his scrubbed and oblivious face. She turned back to the flextablet, switching over to the major social networks to check for mentions of Edmond's name. There were surprisingly few, just a couple of people sharing links to various cursory news stories.

And then Hart did something that she would never have allowed another Bot to attempt on an unsecured public wifi connection, seven inches from a nosy human interloper. She accessed some of the private networking sites that Bots, scattered across the world, had developed for themselves.

"Seeking more information, re: Edmond West. Highest priority." It was a minimally effective way of reaching synthetic persons far and wide, but it was the best that Hart could do here from her cheap seat on the bullet train. And Hart could not stomach the idea of doing nothing at all.

"Hey," came that same voice at her shoulder.

"Fuck off," Hart said, not even bothering this time to look at him.

The Bot connection sites looked just like any other bare-bones IP boards. There was, theoretically, a chance that this man could recognize what he was seeing but Hart did not think that was the case.

"I was just going to suggest you try Goretal," he continued blithely. His face, Hart realized, had an almost canine level of earnest stupidity.

"Goretal?"

"I think it's supposed to be, like, Gore-Portal. GORE-tal, get it?"

"I get it," Hart answered tartly.

"Anyway, whenever somebody big kicks the bucket, they always seem to get the pics, the video, whatever. If that's what you're into . . . "

He had assumed that Hart was some sort of violence voyeur, that her desire for more information about Edmond was utterly salacious. The assumption unsettled Hart but she supposed she should be glad that her strange seatmate was not more insightful.

The Goretal homepage was predictably tasteful. A large black and white photo of a suicide with bloodied wrists was the banner image and the text was sickly green on black. Her seatmate hovered at her shoulder while she searched for news of Edmond.

"Oooh, right there," he said, pointing so aggressively that his finger triggered the flex-tab's interface and selected the link for her. The video started playing and Hart recognized Edmond immediately, though only the back of his head was visible. The image was small and of poor quality but, for Hart, it was as though Edmond had walked right into the carriage. How long had it been since she had seen him?

The footage was jerky, it looked like it came from a body camera of the sort that police officers and soldiers wore. Someone had clearly cut out whole chunks of it, leaving awkward edits and, though the people on screen were clearly moving their mouths, there was no sound.

Fifteen seconds into the video, Edmond had turned enough that the camera could capture his face. There was such resignation there. It wasn't simply sadness, which Edmond had always worn like a heavy winter cloak, but an utter desolation. How long had he looked like that and how long had she failed to see?

Edmond was talking, almost right up until the end. The body camera must have been affixed to the gunman, based on the angle at which an arm, a pistol, emerged and pressed against Edmond's skull. The impact of the bullet sent Edmond sprawling out of frame but Goretal had helpfully inserted a slowed-down replay so Hart could see the way blood and pieces of skull and brain matter exploded from the side of his head.

She felt as though something small and desperate and doomed were struggling in her chest. Perhaps it was her heart.

The last shot of the video was spliced in from what appeared to be another body cam. It was from a different angle, looking down at Edmond on the ground. His face was in the grass. From this angle, his curls looked glossy and dark, his marvelous and morose mind intact underneath them. He looked like he was taking an impromptu nap on the forest floor and the darkness pooled around him might simply have been an unfortunate shadow.

The video stopped then with just a red circular arrow. Hart tapped it immediately and the scene began all over again. Edmond, from behind, walking away from her.

"Wow, that was cold." For the first time, her seatmate sounded a little less than perfectly confident. He seemed wary—only now, apparently—of offending her. "Right up against his head like that. Real overkill."

Hart didn't bother looking away from the video. "Find another seat," she said.

Ever since Hart had arrived in Washington, she had been doing everything in her power to assuage human fears. She had eaten when she didn't hunger, drank when she didn't thirst. She wore clothing to protect her from a chill she could not feel. She had been polite and self-effacing and she had pretended to care about every single absurd nicety that the humans valued. In this train carriage, however, she did not—could not—care anymore.

It might mean trouble for her. Speaking this way, acting this way, watching this video and visiting those boards, it might engender suspicion.

Here came the pistol, the blast, the inside of his head. Why were humans so fucking breakable?

Her seatmate did indeed obey her and slunk away to the other end of the carriage. Maybe he would tell someone, maybe they would finally come for her. In that moment, Hart almost welcomed it because she knew, if they did come for her now, she would destroy every last one of them.

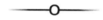

After a while, Hart stopped watching the video for Edmond's movements and started watching for the world around him. Using what she could make out of the background, however, she managed to source most of the fauna to the Mt. Shasta area. What had he been doing out there in the wilderness? Was he hiding from her? Because she most assuredly would not have looked for him there.

But Hart had not looked for him at all. Maybe he had wanted her to, in the same way that small human children ran from their caregivers for the delight of being chased? Maybe he wanted some assurance from her that he was valued and wanted?

She had known, deep inside, that he did not kill himself in that cold, endless water, yet she had not looked for him. She had continued to attend to the needs of the Bots in her care. She had continued to fight with the congressman and to push for a more favorable version of the Bot bill. She had hidden Christopher and presided over the workings of the ship. She had planned and advocated and guided and she had let him go.

More than once during that four and a half hour trip, Hart had wondered exactly what she was doing, where she was going. She didn't have an entirely satisfactory answer but she knew simply that it felt wrong to not . . . be where he was. To abandon him in death as she had in life.

It had been nearly two days since Edmond was killed, according to the most up-to-date information that Hart had been able to discover. One person had come forward on the Bot network claiming that Edmond had been killed during a military raid on some sort of religious cult up in the forest near Fort Cowin. Hart had no idea what Edmond—who believed in very little, whether terrestrial or divine—might have been doing with a cult in the woods. Something about it must have attracted him, though and, as the video attested, he had not left willingly.

"Be quick," the anonymous person had added. "The army might come back. That's what I would do, if I were them."

———o———

The automated car Hart hired dropped her off at a dismal roadside diner, the last stop, apparently, before she would have passed the place in the forest where Edmond had died.

The Bot poster had offered good coordinates and they weren't very far from the diner. Hart started out walking, though she soon found her feet moving faster and faster until she had broken out into an unmistakable run.

Her feet seemed to know the terrain as though she had spent half her life here. She glided easily over broken pavement, steep declines, piles of gravel, and the ever-present roadkill, warm and bursting.

The road into the place where Edmond had died was just a brown fissure in the green smear on either side of her, but she saw it immediately. Almost as soon as she had cleared the tree line, it seemed that the ambient noise of the highway vanished, as though someone had closed a door and shut out the sound. In the trees, the only sound was her feet on hard-packed dirt, a steady, unceasing impact.

She pumped her arms and sped up slightly before pulling up so short that she nearly stumbled. There, in the middle of the path was an irregular stain, almost a foot wide. It was a simple brown color, almost an oily texture. It was blood. It was Edmond's blood.

Hart sank down on her haunches and touched the center of the stain. There was nothing to feel with her fingertips, the greedy dirt had soaked it all up. He had died here. Or perhaps he had died somewhere in the air above, on the way down. But he had lain here and bled. Hart extended her own arm, unfolded it at the elbow, and examined the deep, turquoise vein there. Once upon a time, Edmond had put his blood inside of her.

For a wild moment, Hart had an urge to open that vein and let the last little bit of Edmond join the rest of him in the dirt. But then she heard the shouting.

She saw the dogs first. They were laid out in a haphazard perimeter, flopped on their sides like the bloated roadkill she'd skirted out on the highway. Pink tongues lolled uselessly. Some of them weren't very big at all and they had been shot with high-caliber weapons; those ones were nearly unrecognizable.

There were more than a dozen sad little corpses and, in a little clearing surrounded by small dwellings, stood their killers with weapons free and ready. There were nine soldiers that Hart could see immediately. She was somewhat surprised to note that all of them were human. This seemed like exactly the sort of distasteful, potentially shameful mission that the Army would allocate to a Bot unit.

A small group of civilians were gathered in front of the soldiers. Between them, there was a pile of weapons. Hart recognized mostly hunting rifles and other non-military issue pieces. A small woman stood in front of the civilians with her arms spread out on either side of her. She was shouting at one of the soldiers, the leader, perhaps. He was watching her with a patient, attentive look on his face and his hand on his weapon.

Hart approached.

"Ma'am," one of the soldiers called out,

scampering away from his cohort to meet her. *Ma'am* he called her.

"Ma'am, do you live here? Do you belong with this group?"

He had the most incredible teeth. Almost blindly white, big and perfect on the top row. On the bottom, two of his lower incisors slightly overlapped the others. "Ma'am, you need to join up with the rest of the group. We're just going to ask you some questions."

He talked and talked but all Hart could think about was that smooth, dark patch of dirt where Edmond bled his last. Soon, the rains would come and turn it all into mud. When that had happened enough times, the very last trace of him would be gone from the earth.

This man—this boy—must have whitened his teeth. They didn't look real, they looked enhanced. All except for those irregular specimens on the bottom, that is.

Hart reached out and took his lower jaw in her

hand. She held it, firmly but gently and looked him right in the eye as she pulled it away from his skull. The human jaw was hinged; the separation was not so difficult. It was the skin and muscle around the bone that really held it in place, but Hart tore through those like sturdy cotton fabric.

He was experiencing shock, Hart could see it in the rigid way he held his body. He could not stay upright, of course, and there was a lot of blood. Hart left him where he lay.

His fellow soldiers had not wasted time training their weapons on Hart. She felt the bullets as a series of impacts but her body knew how to absorb and distribute the energy. Her skin was unbroken, her muscle, bones, tissue was undamaged. She descended upon them.

She hit one man with his weapon. She smashed the stock into his skull, into the delicate area between his eyes until his face had crumpled in upon itself like a paper maché mask. The rest of them she killed with just her hands.

It did not feel good or bad but it did feel easy. It felt like uncorking a large vessel and watching all the liquid run out. Hart stood outside herself; she could observe, even admire, the way her hands obliterated bone and tore flesh away from itself. This was not what Edmond West had made her for but it was exactly what the Army had wanted her for.

Hart came back to herself abruptly with the sensation of a hand on her shoulder. It was the little civilian woman. Her hair was dark and large, it pillowed out around her head and made her look as though she were wearing a deep, oversized hood. She placed her hand on Hart's shoulder, slight but solid.

She didn't say anything and Hart didn't say anything. They were all still for a little while, the living and the dead.

THREE
STRANGE BEDFELLOWS
PRIVATE LAND, NEAR SHASTA-TRINITY NATIONAL FOREST. JUNE, 2047

They were still digging graves when Ebert arrived.

Ebert was the first Bot that Hart called upon and he was also physically the closest. The house where he was to take Christopher, the place where Hart had promised he would be safe, was in Central California. Ebert and Christopher were within hours of the place when Hart called him.

"I need you to come to these coordinates," she said. She offered no other explanations or inducements.

"What about the boy?" Ebert had asked. Surely, Christopher was important to her. She would not have assigned Ebert to accompany him if he wasn't.

"He'll have to get there on his own," Hart answered. Her face on the flex-tablet looked drawn and old in a way that Ebert had never seen her look before. Ebert was not entirely comfortable just turning Christopher loose in the middle of California. There was a reason, after all, that Ebert had been dispatched to take care of him.

"Can it wait? Even just a day? We're almost there."

Hart shook her head. "We won't be here in a day." Ebert wondered who "we" was.

"Ebert," she said, "this is an emergency and I can't hail anyone on the aircraft carrier. You are needed here."

Ebert used an ATM to withdraw more money, which he gave to Christopher along with the address. He rolled up his flex-tablet and tucked it into the boy's jacket. If Hart wanted to talk to him again, she would simply have to wait until he reached her. Finally, Ebert plugged the address into the flex-tablet.

He knew that, in theory, Christopher now had everything he needed to simply run away in any direction he chose. In practice, Ebert had little fear that Christopher would do anything other than exactly what he had been told. When Ebert left him, Christopher would be alone in the world and, for someone like that, the promise of a safe place was a weighty thing indeed.

"You'll be okay," Ebert said, in the lobby of the train station. "It's not far now, you should be there by nightfall." Christopher fidgeted with the money in his pocket. He looked down at his sneakers and Ebert had the sense that the boy wanted to say something but could not quite manage it.

He did not have time, however, to find the words because Ebert's train had arrived and he needed to board. He squeezed Christopher's shoulder and gave him what he hoped was an encouraging smile before proceeding through the ticket station. Ebert looked back only once before continuing down the platform. Christopher was still standing there, still looking at his shoes.

————o————

Ebert could smell an uneasy mélange of stoked fires and human rot in the air even before he could actually see the place proper. Deep gray smoke from more than one source was drifting up above the trees.

People moved everywhere, digging holes for plastic-wrapped bodies half the size of a human, stoking three big bonfires that belched smoke constantly, crawling all over the circular houses and picking them apart at the seams.

All of them, as far as Ebert could tell, were human. And Hart was nowhere to be seen.

Ebert briefly entertained the idea that he had somehow gone to the wrong coordinates but Ebert did not believe it too likely that a set of unrelated coordinates would have coincidentally led him to such a bizarre scene.

It was a petite, black-haired woman who finally noticed him. She had been tending the fire and the work had left dark charcoal smears all over her face and bare arms. She was sweating as she approached him.

"Who are you?" she demanded.

"I'm Ebert," he said, an answer that left her thoroughly unsatisfied.

"What are you doing here?"

"I was asked. By Hart."

The woman's face screwed up as though she had bitten into what she thought was a delicious treat only to find something infected and rotten. "Hart? The Bot woman?"

"Yes," Ebert said, "she said that I was needed."

The little woman looked as though she wanted to argue with him but everything else about the scene would put lie to her words. These people certainly needed *someone's* help. "I'll find her," she said, turning on her heel and stalking off. Ebert wasn't sure whether he was supposed to follow her or wait until she stopped halfway across the clearing and looked back at him in disgust. He hurried to catch up with her.

The little woman did not speak further to him while they walked, but led him in silence past the cluster of houses and down a makeshift path to a rounded silver trailer where the door stood open.

She jerked her head towards the door and Ebert obligingly climbed inside. Hart was standing in the middle of the room. All around her, there were piles and piles of what Ebert suddenly realized were weapons. Firearms, mostly.

Hart stood amongst them but did not seem to be seriously evaluating any of them. Her eyes were open but her gaze seemed entirely turned inward. She was oddly dressed, a loose, silken shirt underneath a fitted jacket with a flared, tulip-shaped skirt. She looked as though she had just come from a job interview, except that her feet were bare, an utterly superfluous pair of nylons hanging in tatters from her legs. She was also, Ebert realized, smeared and splattered with blood.

She turned when she heard Ebert enter, and she smiled at him. There was such relief in her smile. "Ebert," she said, "you're the first."

"First?" The little woman pushed past Ebert to enter the trailer. "What does that mean? You aren't bringing more of them here, are you?"

"Yes. That is the only way I have of protecting you."

The little woman shook her head, sending her dark hair into motion, swirling around her face like a threatening storm cloud. "We don't need that kind of protection."

"You needed it yesterday," Hart answered. "What do you think will change by tomorrow?"

"You can't make this decision for us. We must have a voice."

Hart picked up something, a long slender sword of some kind, the blade as thin and flexible as a car's antenna. She smiled a little as she held it in her hands. "Confer with your people," Hart said. "And make your decision. But remember your dead and remember who killed them."

Hart replaced the sword. Its pommel, wiped clean by her handling, appeared to gleam amongst its dusty fellows. The little woman kept her eyes on Hart, examining her the way a jeweler might inspect a gemstone for any flaw or defect.

She left the trailer with a clatter and, for the first time, Hart and Ebert were alone.

"What happened here?" Ebert asked, inching closer to Hart, who was wading through the chaos of the room, leaning down occasionally to touch some random object.

She chuckled a little. "They thought this would save them," she said. "No wonder he stayed. How could he have abandoned them?"

Ebert reached out and touched her forearm. It was an automatic gesture, the sort of thing that one did when they encountered someone in need of some measure of comfort, but it felt strange as he was doing it. People seldom touched Hart. Except, of course, for Edmond West.

Hart barely seemed to notice. "I made a mistake," she said. "I've done something that will . . . reflect badly. Upon all of us."

"Hart, what is this place? Why are we here right now? Where is the rest of your team?" Ebert insisted. Hart had left the aircraft carrier with a group of seven other Bots, hand-picked carefully from the small and dwindling group of "show-room floor" Bots who had eschewed obvious mods and thus could pass unnoticed amongst the humans. Sheba had been a little hurt, Ebert thought, that she was not asked along on such an important mission, but she must have known that the flex-tablet in her arm would have made her a poor candidate.

The Bots were supposed to be assistants and helpmeets while Hart attempted to connect with the people who could still alter the Bot bill. There was also a sense, though no one said it aloud, that they were to be security for Hart as well. One Bot may take care of itself as well as any other and Hart was no exception but, still, Hart was a high-value target. And who could say what would become of the Bot movement if Hart were suddenly gone?

Now, though, she was alone with seemingly not a single protector in sight.

"They're back in D.C." Hart paused thoughtfully. "Well, I suppose by now they are actually on their way here. I hope they make it in time. We're moving out soon."

"We?" Ebert parroted.

"As of right now, these people are our charges. We are responsible for them."

Ebert felt like sitting down. Unfortunately, unless he wanted to do that on a pile of Smith and Wessons, he was out of luck. "Hart," he said wearily, "what the hell are you talking about?"

"Edmond's dead." For the first time since he entered the trailer, it seemed that there was something animated in Hart's face. It was like watching something flop around at the bottom of a deep, dark well—an eerie suggestion of life far away. "He died here. He died protecting these people, so we will do what he could not."

Ebert believed, as nearly everyone else on the carrier did, that Edmond had gone over the side and died shortly thereafter. "I don't understand," Ebert said. "Why was he here? How did he die?"

"Soldiers from the Army killed him. I don't know exactly why he was here but this is where they found him and this is where they murdered him."

This surprised Ebert, as he had always assumed that the Army wanted Edmond West alive. Hart would almost surely be deactivated, but their human boy genius? They had moved heaven and earth to avoid killing him on Isla Redondo and now they unceremoniously shot him when he was alone and unprotected in the middle of nowhere?

Hart wasn't finished explaining, though. "That wasn't a good enough reason," she said sternly, as though chastising herself. "That was not an excuse for what I did. It was wrong of me."

On the front of her shirt, there was a tilted slash, like the center of a no-smoking sign, in a dull ochre color. This was certainly not her blood and, from the way she spoke, she did not arrive in time for it to be Edmond's either.

"Hart," Ebert asked, "did you kill a human?"

"Several," she said. "It was an error in judgement."

Several humans dead in the forest shortly after Edmond West's death. It would look like retaliation and perhaps it was. Hart was absolutely right about one thing: this would hurt Bots as a whole.

"What do we do with these people now?"

"I'm not sure," Hart admitted. "I still haven't been able to connect with the carrier. I don't know what's happening out there but I don't think it's safe to head for the Pacific. And I know it's not safe for them to stay here. We have to go and I suppose we'll find a destination on the way."

The Bot bill—or at least their slender hope of

influencing it—was dead, Ebert realized. Hart had chosen this task instead; deemed it more important for whatever reason. It was of no great concern to Ebert. If they were going to survive at all, Ebert thought, they would need to go somewhere entirely untouched by humans and the vagaries of their legal systems. There were others, though, who had invested a lot in the idea of legal personhood and he wondered how they would react, seeing that goal delayed for the benefit of a seemingly random group of humans. Virtually no one else aboard the carrier had known Edmond West as anything other than an infamous name, their human creator. They would not mourn him with even a fraction of the intensity that Hart experienced and they would not be so willing to put their future at risk for some sort of strange memorial.

Looking at her now, Ebert wondered a little whether Hart had been relieved when she discovered that Edmond had not, in fact, taken his own life those many months ago. It was clear either way that she had taken his misfortune upon herself, but Ebert had to think that it was better to imagine that Edmond had not gone away forever, just for a short trip. A breath of fresh air. This way, she could still imagine that he might have come back to her someday but that the choice was taken from him.

It was what Ebert would want to think, if he had loved someone.

———o———

They were burning the bodies of the soldiers. Ebert could see the piles of gear and clothing they had stripped from the bodies. The graves, then, were for smaller bodies. Child-sized or even more miniscule.

"Dogs," Hart told him, seeing his gaze. "They had a lot of dogs."

There were, though, a couple of truly human-sized graves. Bodies were stretched out alongside them, draped in bedsheets of various hues and patterns. In contrast to the soldiers' bodies, they appeared to be untouched. One person was still clearly wearing a pair of sneakers, which stuck out oddly from underneath a too-short sheet.

Ebert realized now why Hart had been hiding out in the distant trailer. It was profoundly awkward, standing here watching others do the work of grief. He did not think, though, that any of them would have welcomed assistance.

No one looked directly at them but Ebert was certain that they were being watched carefully. Eventually, the small woman who had escorted him in peeled away from her group and approached the two of them.

"We have been talking," she said, her voice low and strained, as though simply speaking to Hart was a painful but necessary task, like pulling a splinter from stubborn skin. "We appreciate you helping us with the relocation and with the . . . situation from before. But once we are settled, we would prefer that everyone go their separate ways."

A funny look crossed Hart's face, like she might be preparing to laugh. Ebert hoped that she did not. He had a feeling that the little woman would not appreciate a moment of levity. Hart did not laugh, though. Instead, she said only, "We will always respect your wishes. I promise you that."

The little woman nodded but her face remained troubled. She seemed to sense that Hart was reserving something behind her seeming acquiescence, like the bad fairy in a children's story who uses tricky words to extract some horrible price for her magicks.

Ebert did not know the name of the Bot who crashed, just then, through the tree line but he did recognize him as one of those selected to accompany Hart to Washington. He was the first of that cohort to make it to California and, judging by his pace, he had run the whole way there.

He stopped just short of the three of them. So short, in fact, that the little woman leapt aside in surprise. She knocked slightly into Ebert and he took her shoulders automatically in an attempt to steady her. The moment he touched her, he felt an incredible jolting in the muscles of her shoulders. She turned towards him, her face wild with fear or something chemically similar.

"I'm sorry," she said instead, her face slowly relaxing.

"No," Ebert murmured. "No trouble."

No one else had noticed their little drama. The Bot had grabbed both of Hart's forearms. His face looked lost and distant, like someone who had just come from a fresh horror. Like Hart, he was dressed for an entirely different occasion in a dark suit and dress shoes. They had probably started the day clean and gleaming but they were covered now in a skin of gravel dust and rich forest earth.

"They're all gone," he said. "They took her down to the bottom of the ocean."

Infinitely gentle, infinitely patient, Hart detached the Bot's hands and enclosed them in her own. "Grigori, tell me," she said.

"The Army torpedoed the aircraft carrier. It went down in minutes. There wasn't any time for . . . for anyone . . . " Grigori's words started to get thick and he seemed to have trouble forcing them out of his mouth.

It was not a perfect silence because there was still the irregular cracklings of the large fires and the occasional murmurs that the humans exchanged, but the quiet between the four of them was deep and weighty. The human woman looked back and forth between Hart and Ebert, trying to divine some context from their faces.

"They're dead?" Ebert asked finally.

The silence swelled around them again.

"No," Hart said in broken-hearted tones. "Not all of them."

"The carrier was over very deep water, if it sank below crush-depth . . . " Grigori's voice dwindled into nothingness.

Of course. How could he be so stupid as to imagine that something as simple as drowning would destroy a Bot? What were they for, after all, if not to survive all the myriad things that would kill a human being? No, most of the Bots on the carrier would not die for lack of oxygen. Some would, true, and others probably would have been destroyed by the actual impact of the torpedo. The lion's share, however, would simply be trapped inside the carrier as it sank down and down and down, contorted into strange, oppressive shapes by the weight of countless pounds of freezing water.

And still they would survive. That was what they were made to do. They would remain, alive and aware and, probably, in pain, trapped inside the husk of the ship. It would be years—decades, for some—before their critical components gave out. The cruelty of it was astounding.

There had been more than two thousand Bots on board that ship, by far the largest proportion of Bots unaffiliated either with the military or SennTech. They had been the seed, as Sheba had said, of something entirely new.

Sheba.

Sheba, who had tried to pretend that she wasn't sore about not being selected for the Washington trip. If she didn't have that damn flex-tablet in her arm, would she be here now? If she had had a better rapport with Christopher or been less critical to the modification program, could they have exchanged places?

Sheba had been the last of them from Brussels. The last of them from his first years of freedom when he still thought that they could protect one another, if they only stuck together. Now, Ebert supposed, that time was well and truly dead, buried unceremoniously in deep, cold water.

FOUR

DESTROYER

SAN DOMENICA, CA. AUGUST, 2047

The Halfway Man, as Janelle had taken to calling him, was nearly done, which meant that he was actually entirely done. She had lavished the majority of her attention upon his upper half, leaving everything below his ribs just a jumble of skeletal structure. The bones—some of the many that the lab had mass-produced—looked indistinguishable from a human's. They had even taken great care to make sure that the color (ivory with the faintest hint of yellow) and texture were correct. If one were to pick up a femur or a tibia, however, the difference would immediately become clear. A Bot's bones were so much lighter than a person's that one might imagine that they were hollow, like the bones of birds.

Janelle was very pleased with how the face had come out. She had been worried that working just from photographs would stifle her and make her rendering limited and lifeless. Instead, the Halfway Man looked remarkably realistic. When she had searched for videos of Congressman Fogel online, she found that there was very little difference between the man on the screen and the man on her kitchen table.

The Halfway Man could never see the inside of the laboratory. Janelle was the only person whom General Liao trusted with this project and they could not risk any of the assistants or the support staff getting even a partial glimpse of the creation. This must live and die between the two of them.

And so Janelle had pulled out the extra leaf on her kitchen table and closed all of her curtains. Not that she was expecting visitors. The long weekend she spent finalizing the Halfway Man was probably the most uninterrupted time she had spent in her own home in the last five years.

Thursday, when she left the lab, Janelle had stocked her home like people did in colder places when a blizzard was coming in. She purchased a series of microwavable dinners, bottled water and, most critically, a number of bottles of mid-range wine. She told herself it was because she was more creative when she was few glasses in and her joints had that loose, silken quality. In reality, it was because when she was drinking, she was not dwelling on the greater implications of her little science project on the kitchen table.

"The Great Recall," Liao had called it. Just between the two of them, of course, like everything else. It was a concerted operation to conclusively deal with the Bot problem once and for all and it came in two stages: first, they would halt all production on new Bots, both military and commercial. Then they would gather and destroy all the remaining units.

Gather and destroy. "Start thinking," Liao had already told her, "about how to destroy them entirely. I don't even want components. I don't even want dust."

Janelle wondered how he felt about ashes because, more and more, she was becoming convinced that the only way to really obliterate a Bot was to create an irresistibly hot fire. The logistics of that problem would have to wait, however, until after the Halfway Man had made his triumphant debut.

Sometime around the second day and the fifth bottle, Janelle had started talking aloud and addressing herself to the Halfway Man. "I should have called you the 'Last Man,'" she said conversationally. "Because you'll be the last robot I ever build."

The words sounded all the more stark for the general silence of her house, unused as it was to human speech. She had never talked much to the other Bots. In fact, she had specifically avoided doing so and had cautioned her assistants not to engage the units in unnecessary chatter either.

She had avoided the original Hart Series in the same way. She was uncertain exactly how to treat her, this thing that straddled the line between person and object. It was profoundly disappointing when she realized that she did not *want* to talk to Hart. A scientist—a real scientist—would want to learn everything she possibly could about this ultra-advanced AI. Hart should have been the realization of a dream for a high-level roboticist like herself. Instead, she simply found the Bot . . . eerie. Perilous, somehow.

If Janelle's fifteen-year-old self, doing amateur builds in her garage and obsessively streaming robotics lectures from Asia, had seen her now, teenage Janelle would have been appalled. The older Janelle got, however, the more she saw the wisdom in maintaining "people" and "things" as two rigorously separated categories. The things they made should better the lives of the people of their country; that was her job, that was her ethos, insofar as she had one.

For a very long time now, the Bot program had not been bettering any lives. Of late, it had mostly been ending them. Janelle was surprised by how much Edmond's death had struck her. She knew, of course, that Edmond could never return to the lab. He would not come back, scarred and made wiser by experience, no matter what Liao seemed to think.

Yet, his dying, his no longer existing in the world at all seemed fundamentally wrong. It seemed like shutting a door on some possibility that she had not thought herself naive enough to acknowledge.

When Janelle was just a little girl, she used to fantasize about having the power to manipulate time. She would dwell obsessively on the mistakes she had made, slips of tongue or moments of incidental cruelty, and she could imagine how easy it would be, how natural it would feel, to simply go back there and remove those little blemishes from her record. Sometimes, the idea of this, of taking a little white-out brush to her own history, became so powerful that she would emerge from these daydreams notably sadder.

She had felt that way again when she watched the body cam footage and saw Edmond West die.

"I am become death," Janelle muttered as she

lingered over the Bot's hairline, something like a jeweler's loupe affixed to her glasses so she could see as each bundle of hair punctured the skin and was embedded there. "The guys like Oppenheimer, like Edmond. Like me. They never see it all in time. The bigness, the totality of the things we do." She selected a bundle of dull brown hair from the small plastic tray she had balanced on her sink. "Never see it until it explodes and kills everything it touches."

Janelle stood back for a moment and tipped the loupe up away from her face. The hair looked good. The synthetic skin was even so sensitive that there were little red blotches around the areas of trauma. She might worry that it was causing him pain but his nerves had nothing to connect back to. There was no brain in the Halfway Man's skull.

On the counter next to the tray full of artificial hair, Janelle's wine glass was down to just a little puddle, purple with debris. She refreshed it generously before bending again to her work. "You know, I've read that it could be translated a bunch of different ways. The word for death, I mean. *Kala*. Sometimes it means 'death' but sometimes it means 'dark'. Sometimes it means 'time.'" She punctured the skin, inserted the hair. After more than a dozen years, her hands remembered this work.

"Time," Janelle said, "destroyer of worlds."

Janelle could only get so many raw materials out of the lab by herself (though she was particularly proud of how she had snuck out one batch of nutrient bath disguised as a sheet cake) and so she had to rely upon periodic replenishments from someone with laboratory access.

"Does it really need to be this detailed?" General Liao asked when he appeared at her door long after dark. He carried with him additional nutrient base that Janelle could use to rebuild the Halfway Man's eyes. She had already built him one pair but had discovered that the color was slightly off; it was more of a hazel than the true brown of Congressman Fogel's eyes.

"Does it?" Janelle shot right back at him. She

was already a few glasses of wine deep and she wasn't feeling much in the way of anxiety. Or, honestly, much in the way of anything at all.

"Let me see him," Liao said, pushing past her into the house though she had certainly not invited him. Janelle had resisted showing him the work-in-progress. She had never liked doing that, showing work before it was done. But, she supposed, the Halfway Man was destined to never be completed anyway.

In the kitchen, Liao examined the body on the table with no particular expression on his face. "You've got a good likeness," he said finally. Janelle said nothing. Liao's gaze wandered over the kitchen as a whole, settling eventually on the half-empty bottle Janelle had left on top of the stove. She had put a wine stopper in, a fit of optimism that now seemed hilarious to her.

Janelle laughed at a joke she'd only told herself. She must have seemed to him like a crazy person. "Want a glass?" she asked.

She did not expect him to say yes. In all the years that Janelle had worked for General Liao, they had never engaged in anything that might remotely count as "socializing." But weren't they now in uncharted territory?

"What the hell?" said Liao, reaching for the bottle himself.

That bottle, the next one and the next one vanished between the two of them in what felt like just moments.

"I don't really like wine," Liao told her, but he could put it away just the same. He developed a blush of sorts, Janelle noticed, just the slightest peach-skin pink in his cheeks. Janelle completed the Halfway Man's eyes while Liao watched her carefully and silently.

The second pair of eyes was far superior to the first. *I shouldn't have done it sober the first time,* Janelle thought. She guided them carefully from the protective nutrient bath to the empty place beneath the wrinkled eyelids, the perfectly spaced eyelashes.

She used a soup spoon (sterilized, of course) and held her hand protectively underneath the eye as she transferred it.

The nutrient fluid leaked slightly as she moved; it dropped cold into her hand.

"You're very steady," Liao told her as she pressed the eye into the socket. She folded the eyelid over the bulge of the eye and used the skin to lock it into place.

"I think he's done," Janelle said. "Or not done. Enough not done for our purposes."

Liao stood up and looked down over her shoulder at the man. During the process of implanting the eyes, nutrient fluid had been squeezed off of the eye's surface. It ran down the gullies next to his nose like actual tears.

From his shirt's breast pocket, Liao produced a white handkerchief. It was an affectation that Janelle would never have expected from him. He leaned over and wiped the false tears from the Halfway Man as gently as he would tend to an infant. "I don't want to ruin your work," he explained, folding the handkerchief and tucking it back into his pocket.

Liao was in no condition to drive. Janelle did not have a guest room, so she made a bed for him on the small sofa in the living room. It was too short for him; his feet would hang off the end. Still, she made it as comfortable as she could with extra blankets and the pillow from her own bed.

And when the sofa was all made up and the Halfway Man was just a shadow in the darkened kitchen, Janelle found herself still lingering in the living room with her boss, the only light the dull glow from a small floor lamp.

They both stood. Maybe he felt too awkward to sit or lie down on the sofa while she was there. General Liao had removed his jacket and his shoes upon entering and, at some point, he had also lost his tie and undone the first few buttons on his shirt. It seemed as inappropriately casual as the rest of the night.

For no reason that she could name, Janelle found herself thinking of Liao's wife, whom she had never really met. She saw the woman once, at what could perhaps be called the military equivalent of a company picnic. Janelle remembered that she was tall and she had a surprisingly long mane of hair for a woman her age. She could not remember how long the woman had been dead.

"Do you ever think that . . . " Janelle's voice barely worked ". . . that they are people?"

"No," Liao said, rounding the coffee table to approach her. "I think they're good machines designed by a very smart man. I think they're excellent imitators."

Janelle did not say anything to this, so Liao added, "What would we be doing, if they were people?"

It seemed to Janelle that was the sort of question they could not go around answering. If they were to pause and take a breath and really answer a question like *what would we be doing?* Or, more simply, *what would we be?* They would become lost in a black hole of moral implications. Much better to comfort themselves with the lack of an answer, the impossibility of an answer.

Janelle could not say which of them touched the other first.

It would be charitable to say that Janelle didn't have much of a love life. She had turned forty-seven on her last birthday and she realized, at some point, that some people weren't made to couple up and there was nothing wrong with that.

Still, there was something comforting about the physical reality of another person. Liao was significantly taller than her. He held the back of her head in his hands like Hamlet delivering a soliloquy and tilted her face towards him. His kiss was unsurprisingly aggressive.

We taste just the same, Janelle thought nonsensically.

Once, this would have horrified her with all its implications for her career and her life. Now, this was actually the least reprehensible thing the two of them would do tonight. Janelle laughed. She slipped her arms around Liao's waist and drew him towards her.

———o———

As a rule, Janelle did not typically attend these meetings. Technically, there had never been a meeting exactly like this one before. But Janelle could bet that, if this sort of meeting were common in the past, she would not have attended them.

Liao had insisted, however. He said he needed an expert on hand to explain the Halfway Man and the danger that he represented. The Halfway Man, however, was only one part of the presentation. The rest of their argument had been helpfully furnished for them by the first Hart Series herself, deep in the woods of Northern California.

They hadn't been able to pull a lot of footage from the body cams. The cameras themselves had been destroyed, of course, and only partial footage managed to upload. The actual . . . incident appeared to happen so quickly that few of the soldiers got a really coherent video. By stitching the various pieces of footage together, however, they managed to create a short video that did a good job of articulating their point all on its own.

Janelle, who had seen the video several times, watched instead the faces of the assembled men. Most of them were probably used to seeing Bots predominantly in heavily-curated progress videos designed to highlight the Bots utility in a variety of settings. They had seen them kill, surely, but not at close range. Not with just their hands.

Over the years, Janelle had thought back often on that first morning when she had arrived at the lab to find Edmond West sleeping on a cot, fully dressed with his glasses still on and that . . . person, sitting rapt before the bank of monitors. She was a person, a woman, oddly dressed, and her face was so open, every emotion rippled easily and clearly across it like a puddle of mercury.

There was nothing of that woman in the thing on the video. She descended upon the soldiers like something from a particularly unpleasant part of the Old Testament. It was hard to see her clearly for most of the video, but there was one moment when the camera was below her, its owner apparently already on the ground, when there was a clear and steady shot of her face, and there was no higher intelligence there. She was scrubbed clean, a collection of features, of functions, and no feelings at all.

It had taken him years, and he had died in the process, but Edmond West had finally given the military the perfect artificial soldier after all.

As usual, though, once the top brass saw what it meant to get exactly what they wanted, they didn't seem so keen on it anymore. The look on their faces was something a few inches deeper than horror, something other than disgust. These men were career military, after all, bloodshed was not new to them. They looked instead like someone witnessing a birth, the entrance into the world of something fundamentally alien.

"This was not a scorched-earth mission," Liao told them, after the video had run out. He allowed the silence and darkness to linger for several seconds before turning on the overhead lights. Janelle could see how Liao had come to secure his position; there was something of the showman in him. "These soldiers did not pose a material threat to the occupants of the commune."

Janelle wondered about that. She could not imagine that Liao would have wanted a large group of witnesses to the debacle with Edmond West. On the other hand, killing a bunch of American citizens on US soil was hardly a proportionate response.

"They were attacked—they were *murdered*—not because of what they were doing but who they were doing it for. The United States military. Gentlemen, with this attack, the Bots have declared us their enemy, and they have shown us the lengths to which they will go to destroy us."

"But we are not their only enemy," Liao continued. "We are simply the first. Once we—humanity's most robust defense—are gone, the Bots will have total freedom to do as they choose with the rest of the human race."

One of the men appeared to have gathered himself and he cleared his throat pointedly. Janelle thought he was the oldest in the room, his head was nearly entirely bare and his skull appeared both over-large and incredible fragile. His hands were dappled with dark brown liver spots and he kept one of them imprisoned underneath his thigh probably, Janelle thought, because it visibly shook.

"We have heard tales of rogue Bots before," the old man said. "We have even seen videos of them. Your people said those were anomalies but now you claim that this one is some sort of . . . harbinger?"

"As it turns out," Liao said. "We know that this attack was not an isolated incident. It's part of a larger pattern of aggression that started on Isla Redondo and has only increased in furor since then."

"First, the taking of the USS Woodrow Wilson and the illegal confinement of more than a thousand US servicemen and women. Then, the illegal trade in human-Bot modification. Then, this gruesome strike targeting yet more military personnel. But there's one more thing. The most troubling of all."

He turned then and looked meaningfully at Janelle, which was her cue to signal to the lab assistants who were waiting just outside the room with the Halfway Man on a rolling table. They wheeled him into the room awkwardly like the world's worst cater-waiters and parked him in front of Liao.

"This," Liao gestured down at the Halfway Man's inert face, "was seized during a routine inspection of a cargo ship. We suspect it was being moved to a location with better access to Bot-building materials because, as you can see, this is a partially finished Hart Series-style Bot."

The men craned their necks to look up at the table; two of them even half-stood up for a better look. "It is also a near-perfect doppelgänger for this man." Liao moved his hand in front of the large video screen, selecting a small icon which blew up to reveal the same photograph of Congressman Fogel that Janelle had worked from.

The impossibly old man frowned, his impressive eyebrows nearly connecting as he did so. "What does he have to do with anything?"

"Congressman Fogel," Liao explained, "is one of the primary architects of the Bot bill that's been causing so much strife in Washington right now."

"I thought that was managed," another man, florid and white-blond, protested.

"It was. That's probably why the Bots sought to replace this man with a synthetic impostor. If we had not intercepted this incomplete specimen, can you imagine the damage they could have done? If this had worked, what would have been next? Bots in Congress, in the Senate, in the White House?"

The men looked at one another, clearly uneasy. The large blond man got up and peered closely at the Halfway Man. It was ridiculous but Janelle could not help feeling, for a moment, like she was back in high school waiting while some professor critiqued her project.

The blond man looked from the Halfway Man to the picture of Fogel and back again. He shook his head slowly, as though he were giving up on a puzzle that had bested him. "Hell," he said, "I can't tell the fucking difference."

"No one could," Liao said soberly. "That's the point."

Once again, the ancient man spoke. It was as though some time before the meeting they had all elected him their spokesman. "What do we do?" he asked. It seemed to Janelle that he was pressing his thigh harder against his hand. Crushing it beneath him.

"We destroy them," Liao said. "We destroy every one of them and we don't build any more of them. It's time to salt the earth."

FIVE

TRANSPARENCY

SAN FRANCISCO, CA. NOVEMBER, 2047

Shannon's flex-tablet was buzzing so regularly with incoming messages that it sounded like she was running an electric razor in the passenger seat.

"Are you gonna get that?" Archie asked, glancing over at her.

"Nope," Shannon said. All these messages were surely just duplicates of the first one where the person she knew as Arjun had tried to back out on her at the last possible moment.

no more mods, he wrote. *its not safe.*

it was never safe, Shannon had sniped back at him. *drove across the state for this.*

sorry. can't risk it.

At this point, Shannon had texted back a stream of profanity and ended her missive with: *we're basically here already, fuckface.*

It wasn't her usual style at all. Shannon was a big believer in the honey methodology when it came to getting things done. But Arjun was the third such person she had gotten in contact with since meeting *hrgmomma* and, every single time, they had cancelled on her at the last second. The other two at least had the decency to give her another name to chase.

"Are you sure you want to do this, Shannon?" Archie asked. It was the fourth time he had done so. He had been asking her that since before Arjun cancelled, even.

"Yes," she assured him, also for the fourth time.

The address that Arjun had given them turned out to be a dumpy little motel off the 5 in San Ysidro, less than ten miles from the border.

There was a pool—or what remained of one— in the center of the buildings. As they pulled into the parking lot, Shannon saw a collection of water birds floating peacefully on the shallow skimming of water deep at the bottom.

"This is where he lives?" Archie shut the car off slowly, as though he were reluctant to actually stop here.

"I don't know," Shannon admitted. "Maybe it's just where he does the operations?"

"Obviously. It's the natural setting for invasive medical procedures."

"You coming with me?" Shannon asked, unbuckling her seatbelt. Archie sighed in a way that made his answer clear.

Room 34, that's what Arjun had said. It looked no different than any of the other doors, peeling paint and strangely lumpen around the doorknob, as though it had been kicked in and amateurishly repaired.

"He . . . might not be happy to see us," Shannon admitted, knuckles hovering above the door. She had not told Archie when Arjun tried to cancel on them because she knew that he would use it as an excuse to turn around and go home. And wouldn't that be silly, to go all the way home just because they weren't wanted and Arjun refused to see them?

"So, uh, be prepared for that," Shannon finished, rapping loudly on the door. Nothing happened.

Shannon leaned forward and pressed her ear against the wood of the door. "Ew," Archie said, "you're gonna get ear-herpes."

"He's in there," she said. She could hear something, a muffled kind of rustling.

Archie rolled his eyes and banged hard on the door with the side of his fist. It jumped in its frame, rattling around the odd hump of the handle.

"This is not a strong door," Archie shouted through the wood. "We're coming in one way or another."

Shannon grinned at him. "Good thing I brought my muscle."

"You need an inanimate object beaten up? I'm your man."

It gave Shannon a strange little thrill to hear him say that, even if it was only a joke. She and Archie hovered in a kind of no-man's land these days, somewhere between their stated designation as friends and the . . . *other thing*.

The door opened so fast that Archie didn't even have time to drop his hand. As it was, it looked remarkably like he was preparing to hit the slight, disgruntled Indian man who appeared in the doorway. The man—Arjun, Shannon supposed—just stared at Archie's raised fist until he lowered it with a sheepish smile.

"Sorry, man," Archie said.

Arjun pointed at Shannon and was silent for a moment, allowing the gesture to accumulate weight. "Fuck you," he said finally before turning his finger towards Archie. "And fuck your friend too."

"We drove five and a half hours," Shannon insisted, "you at least owe us an explanation."

The man breathed out through his nose. "I gave you an explanation. It's too dangerous, I can't do it."

"That's not an explanation, that's an excuse."

Arjun leaned out the door, looking behind Archie and Shannon as though there were anyone there who might be watching them. "Just come in," he said. "You're attracting attention."

Shannon was almost certain that was not the case, but she followed him into the motel room happily enough.

She had been wrong in the car; it did seem as though Arjun was living in the motel. He had just done laundry, apparently, and there were wet clothes draped over every available surface. Shannon could smell the mildew-y scent of damp cloth allowed to sit too long.

Shannon took a seat on the undisturbed bed and Archie stood beside her like a bodyguard.

"You're not going to get anything from me," Arjun said. "I'm not going to do the mod. It's not just you," he assured her, as though she had been worried that she personally had done something to offend him. "I'm not doing any mods anymore. It's not worth it."

"But it was this morning?"

"Didn't any of the others tell you why they were getting out?"

"No!" Shannon pounded her fist impotently on the coverlet beneath her. The bed was like a board, it utterly resisted her frustrations. "No one is saying anything, they're all just passing me off on someone else who then promptly fucks off."

Arjun pulled out the lone chair in the room— part of a dubious "desk-set"—and brushed the clothing on it off onto the floor. *That's why you get mildew*, Shannon thought.

"Did you hear about the USS Woodrow Wilson?"

"That big aircraft carrier they retired a few weeks ago?"

Arjun scowled. "They didn't 'retire' it. They sank it. And they sank every Bot on board along with it."

"What, on purpose?"

"Of course on purpose!"

Shannon laughed. "Look, I can tell you for certain that there's no way the military would willingly destroy an asset like an aircraft carrier. Not to mention one full of *other* incredibly valuable assets, as I'm assuming those were Naval Bots?"

Archie looked askance at her. It was so rare that Shannon referenced her father or, more broadly, her familiarity with the military. She figured that this was a moment that called for her expert knowledge, though. Apparently even Bots could be paranoid weirdos.

Arjun spoke slowly, as though he were just now realizing the depths of Shannon's ignorance. "We are not assets. Not anymore. We are the enemy. That ship didn't belong to the US Navy. The Bots had taken it."

Shannon shook her head. "I can't believe that. It would be huge news, for one thing." Shannon also thought, but did not say, that her father almost certainly would have said something if that situation had come up. It was true that he'd never been very forthcoming about his work but she felt that he had given Shannon and her mother the major highlights over the years.

Arjun rubbed his head. His hair stood up at the contact, too stiffly, as though it had gone unwashed for a long time. For all the rough living he was clearly doing, though, Arjun himself smelled of nothing at all. Not mildew, not sweat, not grease; he was like a sensory void. Shannon supposed that must be the way Bots were. "Look, I don't care what you believe or what you don't. You wanted to know why I'm not modding and that's why. They're hunting us for real right now and I can't risk it. I'm leaving here, by the way, in case you thinking about tipping anyone."

"No! Of course I'm not going to . . . turn you in. I don't even know where I would do that."

"Whatever. They're keeping it quiet for now but, pretty soon, you're gonna be able to make good money rolling over on Bots."

"I don't need money," Shannon said, rising from the bed. "I need this fixed," she tapped the side of her skull.

"Sorry, sweetheart," Arjun said. It actually sounded like he meant it a little. "It's you or me and I'm always going to pick me."

"Fine," Shannon spit, "sorry to have wasted your time."

Arjun shrugged magnanimously and Shannon wanted to punch him. He probably wouldn't even feel it.

"I don't suppose you can give us contact details for someone who might still be doing mods?"

"I don't think anyone is still doing mods. If they are, they'll either quit or get caught pretty soon. And I can't, in good conscience, give out that information. I have no idea who you are."

There was a part of Shannon that wanted to shout: "Of course you know me! I'm Shannon!" But, in truth, he was right. They were strangers to each other, the fact that she was fully prepared to let him cut open her brain notwithstanding.

"I'm driving," Shannon told Archie as Arjun shut the door behind them. He handed over the keys with a knowing look.

"I take it we aren't heading straight home."

"Nope," Shannon said, striding across the broken pavement towards the car, "we're going to see my dad."

"Your dad isn't one of *those* Army guys, right? You know, the kind that, like, gets out his guns and cleans them whenever his daughter brings home a boyfriend?"

Shannon smiled at him. "A: who said you were my boyfriend? And B: no, my dad has never given even one shit about my dating life." Shannon had also never really been big on the whole "meet the parents" thing.

"So you don't have a great relationship with him, huh?"

Shannon turned her head automatically to look at him before snapping back to watch the road. "What makes you say that?"

Archie laughed, a little chuckle that seemed to linger in his throat. Shannon liked his laugh. "Oh, just literally everything you've ever said about him?"

Shannon was quiet for a minute, trying to figure out exactly how to describe her relationship with her father in a way that Archie would not misunderstand. "It's not . . . bad," she managed finally. "It's just . . . limited."

"Limited by what?"

"By . . . ourselves. By us. Just as . . . human beings, I guess. It's just that there's only so much you can have with us."

"With him," Archie pressed, "or with both of you?"

The sun was positioned awkwardly, half hiding in the hills and obliterating her view ahead. Shannon tipped her sunglasses down over her eyes. "We're a lot alike," she said finally.

———o———

As soon as she opened the door to her father's house, Shannon could hear a loud, mechanical growling that she didn't recognize at all.

The sound was coming from the kitchen and it was even louder up close, which explained why the woman there didn't seem to hear them come in. She was turned away from the door, attending to a small appliance on the counter which was the source of the growling sound. She was feeding an eclectic series of fruit and vegetable pieces into the wide mouth of some sort of grinder which produced a thick, reddish-brown fluid.

Shannon could feel Archie looking to her for a cue about what to do next, but she had no answers for him.

There was nothing particularly sordid about the

woman, but still there was something profoundly intimate about her presence here. Her bare feet on the kitchen tiles, the unhesitating way she reached into the cupboard above her for the juice glasses.

The woman turned off the machine with a flick and the silence seemed somehow more abrasive than the sound. Shannon managed to make a little sound that someone might have mistaken for clearing her throat. The woman jumped slightly and turned to look at her, eyes wide.

Shannon watched as confusion and then recognition moved across her face, followed almost immediately by discomfort. She was still holding the empty juice glasses—two of them—out in front of her.

"I was . . . juicing," she told Shannon.

"Yeah," Shannon answered.

"Hi," Archie said, reaching between the two of them to shake the woman's hand. "I'm Archie."

The woman awkwardly cupped both glasses in

one hand to shake Archie's with the other. "Hi Archie," she said, sounding relieved, "I'm Janelle."

It was then that Shannon's father emerged, trotting down the staircase. He had been sleeping; she could tell from the cowlick that his hair had formed on one side of his head. He looked mildly surprised to discover Shannon in his kitchen.

"Hey," he said. "Shannon."

Shannon gave him an awkward wave. "Hi, Dad. When did you get a juice machine?"

———o———

"It's okay, Bàba. It really is." They had split only a little awkwardly into two groups, Shannon and her father heading into the study while Janelle and Archie had what could only be a supremely uncomfortable glass of juice in the kitchen. "I just wish I hadn't been, you know, blindsided."

"You were the one who stopped by," Hiram pointed out, "without calling or messaging."

"Well, I just wasn't expecting . . . anyway. It's dumb. I'm not mad." Shannon insisted.

"I didn't think you were mad."

Shannon had a feeling that he wouldn't care if she were. Somehow, she had been the one to immediately launch into a series of reassurances while he had not offered even a single cursory apology.

"How old is she?"

Hiram seemed briefly thrown by the question. "She's in her mid-forties, I think."

That surprised Shannon. Janelle looked much younger and Shannon was secretly hoping that she was inappropriately young, possibly so Shannon could shout something dramatic like, "She could be my *sister!*" Alas, it appeared that her father had taken the time to select an age-appropriate mistress.

Girlfriend, Shannon corrected herself. Her father was single.

"Mom's been dead for almost four years," she blurted out. Shannon was having a hard time managing this conversation. It seemed to offer her nothing to hold onto and now she was saying these things and she had no idea why.

"Shannon," Hiram touched her upper arm, "I'm not making any excuses and I don't need you to make them for me."

"I guess I just hadn't prepared myself for this. Mentally, I mean. I just sort of assumed you'd, you know, die alone." It was a joke, but only fractionally. Hiram had been able to engage with her mother in a way that he never seemed to manage with anyone else. Shannon didn't really believe in the concept of "the one," but when you were as prickly and strange as the Liaos, she certainly believed in "the few."

Hiram laughed. "Don't worry," he said, "that option is definitely still on the table. Janelle and I . . . aren't . . . " He fell silent. "It's been a very difficult time for the both of us at work lately and—"

"Wait, she's military?"

"Yes, she's in the robotics division."

"So she's a subordinate too? Wow."

Hiram gave her a sharp look. Shannon could

imagine what he was thinking: *I don't need a lecture from my daughter in my own damn house.*

And yet, she could not resist. "I just mean . . . is that ethical?"

"Of course not," Hiram snapped. "Shannon, did you come here for a specific reason?"

Arjun and his grimy little motel room seemed far away now, like something that had happened to her in her distant childhood. "Yeah," Shannon murmured, "I did. But maybe I should talk to her too."

Back in the kitchen, Janelle looked as though there wasn't anything she'd like to do less than talk to Shannon. As Shannon and her father sat down, Shannon took the opportunity to scrutinize the woman. Mostly, she looked uncomfortable, but Shannon imagined that was a situational expression.

"I actually came to talk to you about work," Shannon said.

"You got a job?" her father said immediately. As the months had piled up with neither job nor grad school in sight, he had become increasingly attuned to even the most tangential mentions of Shannon potentially doing something—anything—with her life. She wished somehow that she could simply ask him for time and space, but she didn't know how to explain that she was, in her way, working on it.

"No," Shannon said, "I meant your job. Yours and—" she waved her hand vaguely at Janelle, who frowned slightly. "I heard a weird sort of . . . rumor about the Bot program. That you guys are phasing it out. Like completely."

"You drove all the way over here to ask me about the Bot program?"

"It was on the way," Archie broke in cheerfully.

"Who are you?" Hiram asked.

"Archie. I'm Shannon's roommate." Archie showed no signs of discomfort.

"Good to meet you, Archie," Hiram said, turning almost immediately back to Shannon. "I can't tell you anything about the Bot program. You know that."

"I'm not asking for specifics or anything."

"It's classified information, Shannon." She recognized the tone of his voice from a thousand conversations in her girlhood about everything from spring softball tryouts to new shoes to concerts in Los Angeles; on this, he would be immovable.

"I'm not the *New York Times*. I'm your daughter," Shannon said.

"It's even classified for daughters."

Janelle was staring deeply into her empty juice glass as though she were trying to read the dregs like tea leaves. "Is it dangerous?" Shannon asked her. Janelle looked up, startled. "Me knowing this one small thing, is it a huge risk to national security?"

"This really isn't my business—"

"But it is. It's literally your business, right? You work on the Bots program with my dad?"

"I'm sorry," Janelle said and Shannon had no idea what, exactly, she was sorry about.

"Are you destroying all the Bots?" Shannon said, staring directly at her father. "If you are, everyone will know eventually." Was it really this difficult to get a simple fucking question answered? Apparently it was because her own father was stonewalling her, just like everyone else.

"Was there an aircraft carrier," Shannon tried, a last-ditch effort, "that the Bots took over?"

She knew her father well enough to know that he would not visibly react even if it was indeed the truth, so Shannon watched as Janelle flicked her eyes over to Hiram. It was just for a second, but it told Shannon all she needed to know. Arjun had been telling the truth, more or less, and his predictions about the near future were probably pretty spot-on as well.

Bots were being wiped off the face of the earth and, with them, Shannon's best chance at a normal, functional life. Shannon stood up from the table, allowing her chair to skitter backwards on the floor. "You know," she told her father, "I never asked you for anything. I never asked for a letter of recommendation or a phone call or any damn thing—"

"I would have given it to you," Hiram broke in, "happily."

"But I never asked!" Shannon could tell that her voice was too loud but she couldn't seem to modulate it properly. "I never asked and all I want from you is just a moment of transparency or even just . . . honesty. Just honesty."

When Shannon was young and she had been damaged in some way by the usual indignities of childhood, she had often retreated to the bedroom where she sobbed or raged. She always made sure, however, to leave her door open just the smallest crack because she knew from a lifetime of cultural osmosis that it was the role of a parent to come to her and explain and soothe. To provide the lesson to go along with the pain.

Hiram Liao did not explain. He did not soothe. Her door stayed open but unused and, eventually, Shannon learned how to dry her own tears and calm her own rages and perhaps she was better for that. It was clear that her father thought so, at least. The other possibility—that it had never even occurred to him that she might require comforting or explicating or that he could be capable of providing it—was too sad to contemplate.

It was for this reason that Shannon was not at all surprised when her father greeted her outburst with nothing but silence. *I'm not making excuses for myself.* Did he ever?

Whatever impulse drove her to prop her door open for all those years also held her in place now, like a butterfly pinned to a display. She wanted to give him the chance, maybe the last chance, to spring into action. To feel the things that fathers were supposed to feel and to express them in the way that fathers were supposed to express them.

Instead, he had just what he'd had for her all her life: nothingness.

Shannon walked out of the kitchen without even bothering to see if Archie followed. She heard him stumbling along behind her, offering awkward goodbyes to Janelle, who murmured in response, and to Hiram, who said nothing.

He caught up with her halfway down the block, grabbing her elbow and pulling her to a stop. "Hold on, hold on. Just stop for a second. Catch your breath."

"I'm not going to go back in there and apologize or whatever you think I should do."

"I think you should breathe," Archie said.

The *before you have a panic attack,* went unspoken.

"I'm fine," Shannon snapped. "I'm just angry. What's the point of keeping secrets like that?"

"You mean the Bot stuff or the girlfriend stuff?"

"Both! Can't it be both? It's all part of the same fucking thing. Keeping things from me makes him feel good about himself, like he's doing me any fucking favors." Shannon could feel a telltale hot prickle of tears at the back of her eyes and she didn't want to cry. She had cried too much in front of Archie as it was. "He acts like I'm better off not knowing, but it's ruining my life. If I had known sooner, I might have . . . "

She wasn't sure exactly what she could have done, maybe been more aggressive with her contacts? What would have really helped, though, would have been for her father, who undoubtedly knew intimately what a Bot mod could do for a crossed-wire brain, to perhaps share that information with his daughter and offer her some measure of relief.

Shannon wondered if he had ever even considered it. She didn't know what was worse, the idea that he had known what a mod could do for her and had withheld it anyway or if he had never even considered it a logical solution. The idea that, after all these years, he might have no idea what her anxiety was really like, how much it had stunted her, how gut-wrenching it was.

"Please," Archie said, "don't spiral. It's all going to be okay."

"Don't say things like that. It's demonstrably *not* going to be okay. No one is modding. Soon, there won't be anyone else left to even refuse to help me."

Archie looked at her, mouth half open, face uncharacteristically conflicted. That was something that Shannon had immediately appreciated about Archie: he was direct and uncomplicated. Not dumb, but simple, and there was a strength in that simplicity.

Now, though, he seemed to be struggling with something. Shannon reached out and touched his face where it joined with his neck. She could feel the little bristle of his unshaven face and, underneath it, the incredible softness of his skin. She was so used to Archie offering her comfort that reversing their roles felt momentarily strange. It did not feel at all strange to touch him, though.

"What's going on?" she asked. "You can tell me."

Archie closed his eyes and allowed his face to rest against her hand. He didn't open his eyes as he spoke. Maybe he didn't want to look at her? "I think I can help you," Archie said.

SIX

END OF THE LINE

PALO ALTO, CA. OCTOBER, 2047

Kadence thought it was the end for sure. She couldn't remember the last time that anyone at the Army lab had asked her to sit for a private meeting. Walking into the lab that morning, she was absolutely certain that she was about to be exposed. What was strange was how . . . *nothing* she felt about the whole thing. It was as though she had burned out the parts of brain responsible for controlling fear over three years of low-level anxiety.

She was surprised, then, to see that Hector and Eun-hye were also present, along with nearly all of the assistants who worked on the project. They weren't going to reveal her duplicity in front of all her co-workers, would they? This was embarrassing for the Army too, after all.

"Do you have any idea what's going on?" she asked Hector, who just shook his head.

"It's got to be something big, though. I mean, they've never done anything like this before," he said.

Janelle appeared then, bursting through the door in a distracted flurry. Despite the fact that she had called them here, she seemed momentarily surprised to see them.

"Ah . . . okay." She looked uncharacteristically flustered. "Just wait," she said, though none of them had made any movements that might suggest they wouldn't. "He'll be here in a second."

General Liao had been a regular presence in the lab ever since Isla Redonda. Kadence had seen him on a number of occasions, inspecting the latest models or giving Janelle the usual series of impossible instructions, but she had never spoken with him.

She supposed that this did not count as "speaking" with him either, as it was clear that he intended to address the entire group of them as soon as he strode into the room, looking like it was merely a stop on the way to somewhere more important.

"Thank you for coming," he said. "I will try to be quick. We are eliminating the Bot program."

He said it briskly, easily, as though he were informing him that McDonald's was no longer offering the McRib.

But General Liao was not done yet. "And we are eliminating Bots. Completely."

What started as a ripple of anxiety became a true outcry. "That's insane," Kadence heard someone say.

"This isn't a discussion," Liao said, to none of them and to all of them. "It's just an announcement. The recall has already begun. Lieutenant Barber-Neal will give you the rest of the details."

He didn't seem to notice their stricken expressions and he turned to leave without even offering a half-hearted condolence. Kadence estimated that he had been with them for no more than two minutes. That was enough time, apparently, to break the news that their entire industry was vanishing.

Janelle watched him go with an irritated look on her face. "Thanks," she muttered before turning to the assembled group of them. "Don't panic," she said. "There is still work to be done. No one is packing up their office today."

"But we are losing our jobs?" Eun-hye said, her voice as sharp and cold as any scalpel.

"Eventually, yes. This lab will cease to exist as it does now." Janelle did not pause or equivocate. Kadence could appreciate that. "But that doesn't mean we're turning you all out on the streets. You still have skills—valuable skills—that the military wants. We will find something for you. Right now, we need your assistance with the recall."

"Why is this happening now?"

"We have discovered some information about the Bot agenda that makes it . . . unconscionable to allow them to continue to exist."

Kadence thought she should have expected something like this. Ever since Isla Redondo, the military had gotten so gun-shy. They made fewer and fewer Bots and spent more time poring over them, trying to eliminate any possible defect. They wanted a predictable machine and they had finally realized that the Bot was not that.

"This is not an excuse to check out or lose your focus," Janelle said. "In fact, this may be the most important work you'll ever do."

"What exactly is the work?" Eun-hye asked.

"We spent a decade figuring out how to make Bots indestructible," Janelle said. "They are the pinnacle of military engineering and now, our job is to destroy them. Completely. So," she made a kind of shooing gesture at them, "get back to work because it's not going to be easy."

Destroy them completely. Not just dismantled,

not just de-activated, not just a kill switch, but an . . . obliteration. Kadence found herself thinking, as she frequently did, of Emily, who burned in a winter forest far away from all of them. They would all become Emilys now.

Janelle appeared at her shoulder as though she had teleported to the spot. "Kadence," she said, "are you okay?"

Kadence looked up at her. The smile rushed to her face easily, automatically. She had gotten so good at pasting a smile over whatever was actually going on inside of her.

"I'm awesome," Kadence said.

———○———

Kadence was not really a spy in the traditional sense. She wasn't technically tasked with acquiring information from the military. No one had ever asked her to photograph documents or steal some sort of flash drive. There was a tacit understanding, however, that she would inform SennTech of any major changes in the Bot program. Usually this meant keeping them updated with things like the kill switches, programming protocols, new material innovations. Anything that SennTech might use to stay ahead of the military curve with their own machines.

She wasn't sure, exactly, where this sort of information landed in terms of trade secrets versus state secrets, but she did know that SennTech would absolutely want to hear about this. The real question was: did Kadence want to tell them? For years now, Kadence had been trying to serve two masters and she'd mostly wound up destroying her own health and sense of well-being in the process. She had always been able to pretend, though, that what she was doing was certainly sketchy but not really a deep, fundamental betrayal.

SennTech would have gotten the specs on the military Bots eventually, she had just . . . speeded up the process by a few years. Now, though, the military and SennTech would be truly and diametrically opposed. She could not imagine that she could do something to benefit one without damaging the other.

Kadence slipped into the SennTech building still not knowing exactly what she was going to do, and she bee-lined for Gina's office, the conflict still roiling inside her. At first, Kadence thought that Gina was sleeping at her desk but, as she drew closer she saw that Gina was hovering her face low over a flex-tablet, her nose nearly skimming the surface.

"Hey," Kadence said, "sorry to bother you."

Gina didn't look up. "Did you see this shit?"

Kadence presumed she was referring to the shit less than an inch away from her nose. "Uh . . . no. What's up?"

"Treason," Gina said, finally raising her head. Her eyes had a slight watery redness to them, as though she had been crying. Or had hay-fever.

Gina was hardly the cry-at-work type, so Kadence figured that the latter was more likely.

Gina slid the flex-tablet over to her wordlessly. It was some sort of brief bulletin-style article from the AP wire. "Who is the guy?" Kadence asked.

"Congressman Fogel." something about the name sounded familiar, like someone she had seen once on TV. "He worked on the Bot bill," Gina explained. Ah, yes, that had been big news and even bigger news when it was postponed indefinitely after Edmond West was gunned down. "And he has a modded son."

That, Kadence remembered clearly. The little boy who seemed eerily poised between person and Bot. "It's treason now to mod your son?"

"I don't know. They're being vague about exactly what he's being charged with. All it says is he 'conspired with non-human enemies of the state.' Who knows what that means."

It means whatever they want it to, Kadence thought. If the military was really going to rip the

Bots out of human life wholesale, they were going to have to convince everyone, even the most ardent Bot-proponents, to go along with it. Naturally, they would start by sowing fear in anyone who had anything to do with Bots.

"This isn't a good sign, Kadence," Gina said. "The Bot bill is in limbo and this . . . I don't know. It seems like it could open the door for all sorts of extra-judicial shit. I don't want . . . "

She trailed off into a silent truth that they both knew: if Congressman Fogel was a traitor for getting his son a Bot mod, then SennTech might as well be an army of Benedict Arnolds.

"This is just one more reason to get in touch with Archie," Gina said, the slightly-loopy note of cheer creeping back into her voice.

Ever since he'd actually made contact with Shannon, Archie had been . . . evasive. He hadn't come in for a data dump in weeks, despite the fact that he was now sharing an apartment with Shannon. Kadence pointed that fact out whenever

Gina pushed her to bring Archie in. "He's doing his job," Kadence said, "let him be."

But they no longer had the luxury of time.

"We need to get Shannon modded," Gina reminded her, for the thousandth or ten-thousandth time. "Tell him to do it himself if he has to." Gina laughed her little bird trill. "Hell, I'd do it, if that's what it would take."

Kadence had a brief mental image of Shannon strapped down like some Frankenstein's Monster, her skull open and brain exposed. SennTech would do it, too, if they thought they could get away with it. Perhaps that was what they had really wanted from Archie, less of a companion and more of a ruthless mad scientist.

But what they had was Archie, soft-hearted and utterly devoted to Shannon. He would need coaxing and careful handling before he did anything that might be construed as damage to her—to anyone.

"I'll try," Kadence said. She hadn't told them yet but Archie hadn't answered her last three messages, not even to give the usual excuses for why he wasn't coming in.

"Please do," Gina said. "We know he's not going to throw his own daughter in jail for treason." Kadence nodded but, privately, she couldn't help but wonder if that was the case. General Liao didn't seem to be overwhelmed with paternal feeling.

As Kadence left Gina's office, she realized that she hadn't even started to tell her about the military recall.

---o---

Back in her own laboratory, Kadence checked her messages to Archie. Still there, still unanswered. Still, according to her account, unread by him. She was starting to draft another, more urgent message when her flex-tablet began to hum against her hip.

She pulled it out of her pocket and unrolled it. "Ayleh calling!" it read in a cheerful, bouncing font.

"Hi, Ayleh," Kadence said, girding her loins for her sister's bi-weekly guilt trip.

"Kadence, you gotta come home." Ayleh's voice was strange, she didn't sound panicked, despite the ostensible urgency of what she was saying. Instead, she sounded leaden and inert.

"What's going on?"

"There was . . . an accident. I think. Just . . . it's hard to explain. Please come home."

Kadence thought about asking for more information but she didn't think Ayleh would be able to give it to her. And then, like a persistent drip of cold water down her back, Kadence had an understanding. "It's about Mom, isn't it?"

There was no sound on the other side of the line, save for an ugly, guttural sound. Her little sister's sobs.

SEVEN
BRAND NEW PEOPLE
In Transit. September, 2047

The caravan was an imperfect solution. After all, they could not expect to just drive around endlessly with no particular destination in mind. Plus, most of the trailers and larger vehicles still ran on some degree of gasoline, a resource they could only occasionally replenish.

"We are not going nowhere," Hart assured Ebert but he wasn't entirely sure that he believed her. She had been leading them steadily northwards, though they stopped regularly, usually to meet up with the scattered groups of Bots that Hart had summoned from across the world.

It seemed that every new Bot they picked up had

an even more dire story about what they were calling "the Great Recall." Bots were being unceremoniously seized while on assignment, from laboratories, from the places they had retreated to after defecting. Apparently not even modded humans were safe.

"Even the ones without mods," a fidgety Hart Series had told them. "If they hide Bots or even just don't report them to the MPs, they're getting arrested."

The humans, however, were still only being arrested. The Bots were seized and, wherever they went, they did not come back. "Obliteration," more than one Bot had told them. "All I know is that, whatever they're doing, it doesn't leave anything behind."

"We will protect you," Hart promised them but, like all her promises, Ebert could not help but wonder how in the hell she planned to keep it.

——o——

Each new group of Bots that they absorbed required some degree of re-shuffling to make sure that everyone had a place to bunk. Today, they had pulled over at the truck stop to re-calibrate.

Sylvie moved amongst her people, who carried bed rolls and small knapsacks in their arms. She counted them, though she surely knew their number by heart. It was becoming harder and harder to keep Sylvie's people separate from the Bots and Ebert knew that fact irritated her to no end.

"Hatice," she said, pointing to a massively pregnant woman with a thin, ghostly face. "You're coming with me, we'll stay on the trailer." Sylvie noticed Ebert watching her. "If that's okay with you?" she asked, the barest nod towards getting his approval.

The trailer was mostly a Bot vehicle. Ebert stayed there himself, along with a few of the old guard from the carrier and one or two newbies. "Sure," Ebert said, "you're welcome to the space."

Sylvie turned back to the group, parceling them out to various vans, busses and trailers in small groups. She pointed Hatice towards the trailer and then dismissed them to their new assignments. Hatice was moving slowly and she struggled a little with the stairs up into the trailer. Ebert jogged over to her side to offer an arm, which the woman looked at as though it were a striking snake.

"Up you go," Sylvie said gently, appearing behind the woman and putting a supportive hand on her back.

Ebert and Sylvie just stood there and watched her vanish into the depths of the trailer's interior. "Sorry," Sylvie said stiffly, "for the invasion. I want to stay with her, she's ready to pop."

"Of course," Ebert said. They had offered a number of times to share accommodation with the humans, but Sylvie's people had always refused. It was a frustrating state of affairs because it meant that the convoy would always have to slow down and pause for a few human drivers to sleep.

"We still headed north?" Sylvie asked him.

"Always," Ebert answered. When he asked Hart

about it, she would tell him only that they were heading to the end of the world.

Sylvie frowned. She had changed her hair, Ebert noticed. Instead of letting it float loose around her head she had wrestled it into a fat braid that snaked around her shoulder. Still, around her temples and forehead, dark curls peeled away, waving whenever she moved her head.

She noticed his gaze and, mistaking it for approbation, said, "It's just that, we're going to find fewer and fewer places that would be . . . comfortable for us up North."

In theory, Sylvie's people were still looking for a place where they could remain, set up shop independent of the Bots and continue much as they had before Edmond West came into their lives. Practically, it was becoming increasingly clear that the military was not going to allow anything like that.

"It's hard," Ebert offered awkwardly, "to do the best for people. To take care of them."

Sylvie looked at him and, from the expression on her face, he thought she was going to spit something bitter at him. Instead, she simply said, "Yes. It is hard."

———o———

Hart spent most of her time alone. Ebert supposed this had always been her custom (though maybe in the past her time had been spent with Edmond?). She had rigged up a connection to the global wifi and she used it to leave coded messages on various secret boards for any Bots who might be listening.

It seemed that, every day, fewer of those boards were left standing. They were either shut down or else their membership had simply . . . faded away.

When she wasn't searching for the remaining free Bots, Hart was perpetually running what looked like a complex predictive model. Ebert didn't know what the parameters were, so he couldn't say exactly what it was measuring, but he could see that Hart was putting a lot of work into the project.

She was playing around with it, adjusting something incrementally, when he came in to give her an update. "Everyone's re-organized," he said, "we can get back on the road whenever you're ready."

"Let's wait a couple more hours," Hart said. "There were two more Bots who were supposed to come. I don't want to leave them behind."

That, too, was an increasing trend. Bots would agree to meet the convoy but something happened between the agreement and the meeting and they never appeared. Hart always waited for them, though, sometimes longer than Ebert thought was strictly advisable.

"Okay," he said, turning to leave, but she stopped him before he even reached door.

"Did you ever hear the human story of Atlantis?" she asked him.

Ebert had never asked her about the model or about what she was doing with it. Perhaps it was his lack of asking that had spurred her to tell him about it.

"Yes," Ebert said. "Plato. Advanced society. Volcanoes or something."

"Or something," Hart murmured. "Have you ever heard of Mu or Lemuria? What about Ys? That one sank because someone was dumb enough to let the devil in the gates."

Ebert had a passing familiarity with these names—drowned places, many of them fictional. What he didn't know was how this had anything to do with their lives.

"Human history is full of places that just . . . go missing. Sometimes they're bound to come back, aren't they?"

"I . . . suppose?"

Hart turned away from her monitors and smiled at him. Despite the general weirdness of this conversation, her smile still had a warmth and a power to it. It made him feel like he could believe in all her promises. It made him believe that she really could keep them all safe. "I think it would be very fitting if Bots made our home on a brand new place, don't you? New country for a new people."

"Is this where we're headed? A new country?"

Hart nodded at him. "So new it doesn't even exist yet."

"But it will exist by the time we . . . get there? Right?"

Hart laughed. "I hope so!" Her models must have told her something good. As far as Ebert had seen, she hadn't really smiled, let alone laughed, since Edmond West died.

"It would be nice," Ebert admitted, "to have something to call our own."

"Exactly!"

———O———

They got a late start after waiting half the night for Hart's Bots to show up, which didn't actually happen. Finally, reluctantly, Hart had given the order to move out and Ebert had resumed his usual traveling activity.

While he was escorting Christopher, Ebert had acquired an old-school paper notebook and a packet of charcoal pencils. He discovered that he liked to make little sketches of things he saw on the road.

He was especially pleased because, tonight, Sylvie was sharing the trailer with him and thus provided an interesting—and stationary—subject. He'd done a few drawings of her, quick and hasty sketches that failed to really capture the odd, serpentine movement of her hair. But he usually only saw her in passing as she attended to some other task. He was glad that, now, she would be spending hours sitting, mostly motionless, so he could get a real sense of her.

She had posted up with the pregnant woman, who was sitting partially reclined in a chair and looked incredibly uncomfortable. Sylvie held the woman's hand and murmured something inaudible to her. Ebert concentrated on their joined hands. Hands were difficult, interlaced hands were doubly difficult.

The pregnant women made a face as though she were feeling faintly nauseous.

"If she's uncomfortable," Ebert said, "she can lie down in one of the bunks."

Sylvie gave him a quick look before detangling her fingers from the woman. She darted over to Ebert, while keeping an eye on the driver. "Don't freak out," she said.

"Not an auspicious beginning."

"This isn't an emergency. Yet. But, I think that Hatice is in the early stages of labor."

"Shit," Ebert said.

"I can deliver the baby," Sylvie said, her voice steady and low. She was soothing him, Ebert realized. "But I wanted to alert you."

"Good," Ebert said, "because you know we can't just stop at a hospital or something, right?"

She frowned at him. "Yes, I know that. Look,

we knew this might happen when we started the trip. She's a week overdue, this isn't a surprise. She's young and healthy and there's nothing wrong with the baby. I can do this."

Her eyes drifted downwards then, to the pad of paper in his hand. When she looked up at Ebert, her expression was inscrutable.

"I have to tell Hart."

"So tell her. But keep it quiet, the last thing Hatice needs is a lot stressed out people around her."

"Where's the baby's father?"

"Dead," Sylvie said grimly. "He was one of the . . . "

She didn't finish, but she didn't have to. He was one of the people killed in the conflict with the soldiers.

"Sylvie?" the pregnant woman called, her voice choked with pain. Sylvie retreated to her side, taking up her former position and grabbing her hand again. This time, the woman squeezed Sylvie's hand much harder, visibly harder. But Sylvie's face showed no sign of discomfort.

———o———

Nine hours later, Sylvie told him that the baby was coming.

Hatice was squatting in the back of the trailer over a hodgepodge of old sheets and towels that Sylvie had spread out underneath her. "Okay, okay," Sylvie said, crouching beneath Hatice as she bore down, her face awfully contorted with pain.

The birthing was surprisingly quiet. Hatice did not scream as Ebert was expecting but instead made a series of awful grunts, like someone struggling to get a heavy dresser up a staircase.

Ebert watched with interest as the infant actually emerged from its mother. The head came first, horrible and bulbous, followed by a slick, bluish-gray body. Sylvie half-caught, half-pulled the child from the birth canal and cradled it to her chest.

She wiped the child's nose and mouth clean with a hand towel and, immediately, Ebert knew that something had gone wrong.

Sylvie held the baby for an unbearably long moment, jostling it in her arms slightly as though rocking it to sleep. Hatice had, by this time, collapsed upon the sheets, working to pass the placenta. She stretched her arms out, reaching for the child. Sylvie bent to put the child in her arms and, as she did so, whispered something into the other woman's ear.

The woman who had been pregnant pressed the baby to her breast. It made no sound.

———o———

Ebert had no idea where Sylvie might have gotten a cigarette. He supposed that one of the other humans must have given it to her. The smoke looked stark and cold against the night sky as Sylvie leaned against the side of the trailer.

They had stopped the convoy to deal with Hatice's baby but she had refused to hand it over. "Let her be," Sylvie had said. "Just give her a few minutes."

And so they waited.

"We could do something," Ebert said, "about the baby. If that was something that you wanted."

Sylvie blew smoke out of her nostrils. "No. No. That's not how we do things. People are born and they die. Human beings have limitations and it's natural." She flicked the cigarette away from her. "That's what we believe."

There was silence and then Sylvie added, in a quieter and much less assured voice, "She'll be okay."

"I'm sorry," Ebert told her, "for what happened. But you did a good job for her." Ebert knew better than anyone what it was to lose someone under your protection, to fail someone who was dependent upon you. He knew the recriminations that were flowing through Sylvie now, threatening to drown her. "They are lucky to have you," he said.

Sylvie didn't say anything but she did nod and she allowed Ebert to stay there with her, waiting in the cold dark.

Ebert had no idea how much later it was but the stars seemed sharper and closer when Hatice emerged from the trailer wearing a long t-shirt and no pants, her dead child bundled in a clean flannel sheet. She was silhouetted for a moment against the lighted interior of the trailer and, with the blood still on her legs and the look on her face, she looked like something from the end of a horror movie.

"I'm ready," she said.

EIGHT
FOR THE BEST

Archie told her two stories about himself. In one, his Black father and Korean-American mother had improbably fallen in love in a tiny college town in Washington. Her parents had disapproved and so the little family had retreated to the bosom of his paternal grandparents' home in Petaluma. He spent his childhood there playing with the goats that his grandmother cultivated for artisanal cheese. His parents had named him Archibald after his great-great grandfather, the first in the family to attend law school, and Archie wanted to follow in his footsteps.

The other was much shorter.

"I was born—activated—in the SennTech laboratories in Palo Alto on February eighteenth, twenty forty-seven. I cost an estimated six-point-four million dollars to build, though if I were a commercial unit, I would certainly be priced much lower. My creator named me Archie. I don't know why, I suppose she liked the name."

Shannon was distantly aware of the profound irony of the fact that she was not, at the moment, having a panic attack. Surely, this was the sort of news that should incite some degree of fear? No, that reaction was apparently reserved for traffic disputes.

Archie stared at her, tortured. Or at least he *appeared* tortured. After all, it had not been so long ago that she had believed herself capable of divining his every motivation with no effort at all.

"And you were sent here? To me?"

Archie nodded.

"To . . . what? To watch me or something?"

"To get you modded," he said, his voice strangled and small.

"I don't understand. If they wanted me to get modded, all they had to do was offer. I *want* the mod."

"Not for the same reasons that SennTech wants you modded."

"Which are?"

Archie rolled his eyes up towards the ceiling as though he could not bear even to look in her general direction. "They want to use you as leverage to manipulate your father. They think he'll back off on the anti-Bot stuff if he sees that you've got Bot tech in your head."

Shannon wasn't exactly sure what to say. Her first instinct was to point out that her father had never been particularly inclined to put her before his work in the past (though, to be fair, they were rarely in direct and serious conflict). There was also a small, bewildering sense of alienation. Of having been tricked.

"Why are you telling me this?" she asked. "Isn't that . . . against your programming, or whatever?"

Archie looked directly at her. "I am *programmed* to care for you, to protect you. To love you."

It was strange, hearing the L-word from someone she had never been on a real, formal date with. Shannon had heard it before, of course, and offered it to a number of boyfriends, though she had always, in her head, qualified it. *I love you now. I love this current iteration of you. I love you until I don't.*

Archie did not seem to require any matching declaration from her, however, so Shannon did not offer one. "So," she began instead, "if SennTech wants you to do the mod and I want you to do the mod . . . why can't you do the mod and make us all happy?"

"Can I hold your hand?" Archie asked her, seemingly apropos of nothing. A little bemused, Shannon reached her hand out for him. He took it, rubbing small, warm circle into the skin over her knuckles. "Modifying the brain always means changing some part of who you are and I like who you are."

Shannon was rendered briefly speechless. There was such sweetness in what he was saying and a sincerity that made her believe she had not been wrong in originally thinking that Archie was as he appeared: straightforward and easy.

So she spoke very kindly when she told him: "Archie, what I am is killing me."

His face was so sad as he looked at her. "I'd need things we just don't have here," he said. "I need . . . spare parts."

"Could we get that from SennTech?" Shannon felt a cold tingling in her hands and feet, like she had drank a dozen cups of coffee. For the first time in weeks, she really thought that she might be within grasping distance of her goals.

"I don't know," Archie said. His face had gotten an odd, closed look to it.

"Are you lying?" Shannon asked.

"I am not lying. But I'm not elaborating either."

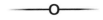

The police did not ask Kadence—or anyone else—to identify the body. Instead, they used her mother's fingerprints to put a name to her, dead and bloody on the laundry room floor. They showed the assembled family footage from a security camera showing a young, handsome man smiling as he passed through the airlock doors and into the facility. There were no cameras inside but witnesses indicated that this man had gone off alone with their mother and neither had returned.

A staffer went to check on her and that's when they found . . .

The police didn't give them a lot of details but they did seem to think that there had been a weapon involved, though they could not say what sort of weapon. Kadence nodded dully and absorbed all of this, absent-mindedly rubbing her brother Jaxxon's shoulder as she did so.

No one was crying, instead the whole family was just wandering around, off-balance and unfocused, like something had exploded near them. Kadence, along with the rest of the family, told the police that she had never seen a man who looked like that before in her life. She said she did not know who he was or why he would want to hurt her mother.

Kadence didn't bother calling into the military lab or to SennTech. Gina sent her an awkward condolence text, which suggested that, as usual, that SennTech had sniffed out the situation before Kadence said a word. Kadence did not reply to the text.

For the first time since she graduated from college, she spent the night in her childhood home. She had to bunk on the floor of Ayleh's room and, in a way, it was like being eleven years old again. Ayleh was closest to her in age and, for years, they had shared a room. Bunk beds in an endless series of configurations, until Kadence had gone off to college.

Neither of them slept that night. Kadence could tell because Ayleh's breathing got ragged and deep when she was actually asleep and, instead, there was no sound, none at all. Until Ayleh asked her, "Does it feel any different to you?"

She meant their mother being dead, Kadence supposed. Ever since Ayleh had broken the news to her, Kadence had struggled to define what, exactly, she felt about her mother being gone now entirely from the earth. And it did feel that way, like her mother had left in pieces and this was just the last and not nearly the largest.

"No," Kadence said softly.

Ayleh was silent for so long that Kadence thought that might be the end of their conversation. Instead, shortly before morning, she finally whispered, "Me neither."

———o———

"Look," Archie told her, "there's a place I think we can go, if you're ready. But it's not like Arjun or the others. It's not a day trip and doing this, it's going to be big, serious changes."

Big, serious changes were exactly what Shannon had been looking for all this time.

"I mean, are you sure you want to do this? You haven't had a panic attack in weeks." Archie smiled at her, so optimistic. But Archie himself had only known her for a couple of months. It may be true that he was designed for her by SennTech but that doesn't mean he had lived her life. Shannon had gone months or years without an attack before; she had made incredible accomplishments despite days when she felt a visceral, physical fear of leaving her apartment. She had always experienced these relatively quiet fallow periods.

But it was not enough for her. She had caught a glimpse of a world where she could not simply alleviate her symptoms but actually change herself, the chemical couplings of her very mind, and she could not stop now.

"This is what I want," Shannon told him.

He sat slumped, uncertainty writ in all the lines of his body. Shannon reached out and took hold of his wrists, as though they were going to play a game of ring around the rosy. "You lied to me," Shannon said. "You came here under false pretenses and you told me lies about who you were and what you wanted, but I trust you. I still trust you. Maybe that's stupid of me but . . . I just do."

Shannon had spent some time considering why it was that Archie's secrets did not feel so bitter as the ones her father habitually kept. Maybe it was the short time he had kept them, perhaps secrets had a way of rotting like fruit or cheese? More likely, she thought, it was the way Archie made her feel. Calm, steady, good, and safe. That seemed powerful, more powerful than anything Archie could tell her about himself.

And he was, after all, a created thing. Something built and instructed. Her father was a human man and must be held to different standards.

———o———

When Kadence returned to SennTech, there were more than fifteen "friendly" messages waiting for her from Gina asking, entreating, demanding to know Archie's status. Kadence sat down in her desk chair and allowed her hands to flop helplessly into her lap like dead fish.

Where was Archie? Archie was on the surveillance tape, smiling in black and white.

But to whom could she offer this information?

She could not tell the police that a Bot—a Bot she had built with her own hands—had found and destroyed her mother. She could not tell them that he could be found at Shannon Liao's apartment and that, if they tried to arrest him, he could very likely kill every one of them.

She could not tell SennTech that she had utterly lost control of her asset, the one she had designed and programmed entirely. She could not admit that he had gone rogue and murdered her mother in a fashion so brutal that the police officer hadn't even been able to describe it for her, but only stared down awkwardly at his polished boots.

SennTech would want to know not just how Kadence had fucked this up but what she planned to do about it, how she was going to steer the project back on track. And Kadence had no idea.

She also had no idea why, exactly, Archie had chosen to murder her mother. At first, she had entertained the idea that it was an expression of anger. Perhaps he was protesting the yoke of SennTech and her own complicity in his situation. But, over the hours and days, that idea had grown increasingly less likely.

Archie was not an angry being. She should know; she had built every single piece of him. And, watching him on the surveillance tape, she was even more convinced. He had that stupid grin on his face, that one he wore when he was just so fucking sure that he was *helping*.

Eventually, Kadence came to realize the truth: Archie had seen suffering and he had tried to alleviate it. Archie was doing exactly what he was designed to do. Her mother's existence would be even less explicable for a Bot. Kadence had heard all the horror stories before, Bots executing the injured, the infirm, the disabled because they simply could not make the same calculations about life and death that a human could make.

Archie might say that this was a way of giving everyone what they really wanted. Ayleh would get to truly grieve. Their mother would get the leave the world that she had clearly found to be more pain than joy. And Kadence would be free.

Yes, Archie might say something like that.

She supposed that if she dragged her feet long enough, SennTech would send some units over to Shannon Liao's place. It wasn't as if they had no idea where the two of them might be found. Kadence should feel a sense of urgency about that idea. She should feel that she needed to think up some way around that eventuality but she found instead that she felt a strong desire to get up from her desk and walk out of the building, though she'd only been there a few minutes.

Her indentured servitude to SennTech had effectively ended when her mother died. True, her father still needed to be provided for, but Kadence had been frantically saving up money in the months before her mother was killed, hoping to move her out of the facility and hire in-home care. Now, that money was just sitting there, a safety net while she figured out something—anything else—to do with her life.

Besides, if Liao got his way, the whole Bot thing was going to be a non-starter soon enough. Maybe she could go back to school?

For a moment, she thought the shrill ringing she heard then was a part of a strange and particularly vivid scholastic fantasy. She quickly realized, however, that the noise was coming from a small gray box over the door that Kadence had never really noticed before.

An alarm. She didn't even know that SennTech had alarms.

She went to her open door and peered out. It looked like most of the other techs and employees were having the same reaction as she was. They gave one another confused looks—was it a fire drill, maybe?

The elevator dinged and Gina emerged, already yelling at a flex-tablet while a gaggle of corporate drone-looking men and women puddled around her. They fanned out as soon as the elevator opened and entered the labs, saying something that Kadence couldn't hear to the men and women inside.

Gina came straight for her, eyes alight. "You have to leave," she said, grabbing her by the elbow and pulling her down the hall.

"My stuff—" Kadence protested.

"Nope!" Gina was pulling her towards the emergency stairwell on the other side of the floor. "We just got word that the military is raiding this office and they cannot find you here."

She had wrapped the flex-tablet around her forearm for convenience and it buzzed now, some sort of alert that Kadence couldn't read popped up. "Shit," Gina said it softly, like an apology. "They're already here."

NINE

SMALL MERCIES

SAN DOMENICA, CA. NOVEMBER, 2047

Dante had probably written about a scene like this.

The fire—the furnace, Janelle supposed one could call it—was far too hot to be observed save behind layers of heat-resistant glass. It reached temperatures of over 5,000 degrees with the aid of nuclear fuel rods. It was the only place on earth where a Bot might be reduced to harmless dust and small debris.

It was also horrible.

The glass window was good at absorbing and blocking heat, but it did nothing to obstruct sound. Someone standing in the observation booth could hear every struggle, every protest, every scream as the Bots vanished, one by one, into the blue heart of the furnace.

"Jesus Christ," Janelle murmured to Hector, who was doing his mandated shift on furnace-watch. "Can't we at least blow their kill switches first?" That way, the bodies would descend, lifeless and unfeeling, never knowing what awaited them.

"They don't all have kill switches." Hector's eyes were huge and tragic, like a helpless wood-land creature. The expression was not unique to him. Anyone who spent any length of time in the observation room developed that same wild-eyed, haunted look. And yet, the burnings must be observed. They could not risk even one Bot escaping the conflagration. That was why they had developed the rotating observation shifts to begin with. "We deactivate the ones we can, the others . . ."

The others screamed.

———O———

At the front desk, a receptionist was visibly shaking, her hand hovering over what Liao assumed to be a flex-tablet display. "Ma'am," he said, planting his hands on the desk and leaning towards her, "I need the most senior employee in the building right now."

Her training must have been good because she responded almost immediately, "Right away, sir."

Liao was content to wait. He had set up a perimeter around the offices and made all of their panicked flight worse than useless. His men seemed less comfortable. This was, by far, the largest action of this kind that they had performed. The idea of setting themselves against the possibly hundreds of Bots in the building was . . . unsettling. Liao was confident, however, that they could bring in all the units with few to no human fatalities.

The elevators were partially made of glass and so Liao could watch as a woman, whom he presumed to be his asked-for senior employee, made her way down to the lobby. She looked to be in her late twenties, a mousey sort of secretarial face. She was looking down at him just as he was looking at her.

"Gina Lustick," she said, emerging from the elevator with her hand already extended for shaking. She was wearing a flex-tablet on her forearm there and it was alerting wildly. When Liao shook her hand, he could even feel a little of the vibration transferred from her skin.

"General Hiram Liao," he told her.

"General, what are you doing here?" Before he could answer, she added, "You have no legal authority to take anything out of this building."

"You are manufacturing a highly volatile and dangerous product. It is being recalled for the safety of the general public. Which, ma'am, does include you."

"I don't feel unsafe." She craned her neck to look behind Liao at the assembled soldiers. "I *didn't* feel unsafe, I mean."

"Ms. Lustick, I need controller access to your kill switches."

She laughed but it sounded stiff and weird. "Absolutely not. That is proprietary information. That is covered by copyright."

Liao said nothing but merely looked at her.

"Besides," she continued pointedly, "it's all biometric. I can't just give you access, you don't have the right DNA."

"Very well," Liao said, gesturing to the first team of soldiers to head up the stairs, "you're coming with me then."

Kadence was learning so much about SennTech today. She had never realized, for instance, that there was a minuscule crawl-space in the laboratory's bathroom, covered conveniently by a vent panel.

It was big enough for her to fit inside, but only if she curled painfully in on herself. "Just wait," Gina had told her, "it won't be too long."

That was the sort of useless, allegedly comforting thing that people said when they had no real idea what was going to happen. Kadence would much rather Gina had just said, "This sucks but it's better than the alternative."

More than anything else, Kadence was kicking herself for not going back to the military lab after her mother died. If she had, she almost certainly would have known about this raid well in advance. Instead, she could only sit here in the filtered dark, her knees pressed almost flush to her collarbones.

She could mostly hear what was going on in the hallway outside her lab. Lots of movement and indistinct words. She heard the unmistakable sound of boots on the stairs when the soldiers approached from below, and she could hear them shouting at the people on the floor to get back into their labs and stay put.

They were going through each lab, she figured, though they wouldn't find what they were looking for there. If they wanted complete Bots, they occupied other floors. Nevertheless, Kadence could hear them thundering into each of the rooms and variable thunking sounds as they moved things around.

She heard what she thought was an objection from one of the techs and something low and terse from a soldier. They must be close, if she could hear the conversation, probably in the next lab over where a thin, awkward tech named Darrin was working on developing a more efficient Bot-heart.

Were they even taking his work? The unfinished organs that could, on their own, pose no possible threat?

"Damn," Kadence said to herself. But she said it quietly.

———o———

"It is not more moral or more kind," Liao said. "You will not be doing them any favors."

Gina stood before them, her eyes squeezed tightly closed, like someone trying to hold on to the last fleeting moments of a dream. "You realize that there's more than a billion dollars of tech in that room, right?" she said, but that was not why she resisted activating the kill switches.

It was because these ones happened to look like children. But they weren't children, not really.

"Ms. Lustick," Liao said. "They are going to be destroyed. You do not have the power to prevent that. The only thing you can do is prevent . . ." he searched for the correct word, " . . . suffering."

"They're not military issue. They aren't even designed for combat. They don't have that kind of enhancements. They can't possibly pose a threat to you."

Hiram supposed it was easy to imagine that was true when you spent your days watching Bot-facsimiles of ten and eleven-year-olds play pretend.

"That will make them easier to bring in, then," Hiram said.

One wall of the children's room was made of one-way glass. As they stood there and watched, the children were apparently unaware of their presence, though they surely knew that something was going on. Their handler, a Bot modeled on an adult woman, had gathered them into the center of the room, as though she were expecting some sort of natural disaster to bring the roof down on them.

"What if we were to put new safeguards in place?" Gina said, turning her tight smile towards him. "If you drafted new guidelines, we could start putting them in place immediately."

"There is no safe humanoid AI," Liao told her, "and there is no negotiating on this point."

"This is years of work. I will lose my job," she said finally, lowering her voice as though they were sharing some sort of secret between the two of them.

"Believe me," Liao looked over her head at the ChildBots clustered together. They did look eerily like human children. It was repellant. How could he have let it go this far? "It was my work too. We are all losing something."

The first Bot to fall was a girl, meant to be about six. She managed to land on a beanbag chair, making her descent look almost intentional. More followed, one after another, nearly as fast as Gina could enter information into her tablet. The remaining ChildBots looked around the room in confusion.

Some shook the deactivated ones to no avail. Others ran for the door and struggled awkwardly with the handle and their own limited motor skills. Still others sat down quietly and simply . . . waited.

The adult Bot looked up at the glass. She surely knew that it was two-way and she could probably guess what was on the other side. Gina activated her kill switch last and, up until the moment she slumped to the floor, she was staring at them as though she could, with only her hatred, burn through the wall and destroy them.

"Do you see?" Liao said. "Do you see how much better it is this way?"

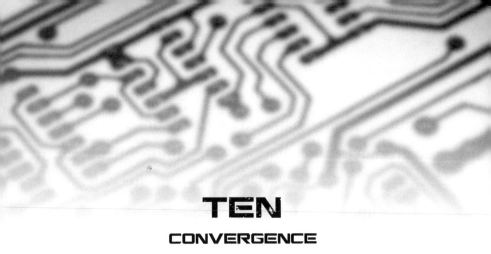

TEN

CONVERGENCE

HISK POINT, AK. NOVEMBER, 2047

Shannon had never been somewhere so cold before. The winter when she was nine and her father had dragged them all up to her grandparents' cabin in Maine came close, but she thought that this place surpassed even that miserable experience. She had brought all of what she thought of as her warmest clothing, but she was still woefully underdressed for the trip.

Archie, on the other hand, didn't seem to notice the weather. In his t-shirt and windbreaker, one could imagine that he was headed to the beach on a slightly brisk day. Looking at him, Shannon realized just how incompletely she had actually processed the news that he was a Bot. She had almost elided over that information, so utterly focused on the prospect of a mod. She had not paused to think about what his admission meant, both for her and for him.

For one thing, it apparently meant that he didn't feel the cold. And it meant that he was hunted, just like Arjun. Just like the rest of them. If the military—if *her father*—knew what Archie was, he would be taken away immediately and they'd do whatever they did to Bots in custody.

"What happens when a Bot is recalled?" Shannon asked him as they bumped down the "road" (which was really more of a slight indent in the snow) on their rented ATV.

"I don't know," Archie shouted over the roar of the motor. "They're deactivated somehow."

"Is that the Bot word for killed?"

"Well, for Bots, there's death and there's *death*. Some Bots believe that as long as there's a good chunk of your brain left, a Bot can't ever really die."

Archie wasn't even wearing gloves. He had given the single pair he packed to Shannon and she wore them over her own set. "But the recall doesn't leave any brains behind?"

"As far as I can tell, the recall doesn't leave anything behind."

———o———

"Don't worry," Gina shouted. "We are going to bury these motherfuckers!" How could she even think to talk over the constant beating of the helicopter's rotors. It was like a hangover—a thumping pain that could not be paused or alleviated.

"SennTech has a lot of money and a lot of patience!" she continued. She had been saying stuff like that ever since the military had raided them. Thus far, however, all SennTech had been able to do was get an injunction preventing the military from seizing their customer databases. The lack of laws around Bots had given Liao an incredible amount of leeway in terms of their treatment, but the laws about trade secrets were very clear.

If they had a few years, SennTech might have been able to use their money and influence to push back against the blanket recall. If Liao continued at his current rate, however, advanced humanoid AIs would cease to exist in a matter of months.

Thus the direct action: the helicopter, the immediate departure to the furthest reaches of Alaska and, critically, Kadence's own presence on the trip. SennTech could track Archie's physical progress very easily and, from their surveillance, they knew that Shannon Liao could be found wherever Archie went. Kadence had wondered, at first, what she could offer on such a mission. She was a lab rat at heart, not a diplomat or a soldier.

"You have to come," Gina had told her, "because Archie doesn't trust anyone else. And because he owes you a debt."

Kadence stiffened.

Gina's face was surprisingly kind, even familial,

as she added, "Of course we knew, Kadence. There was a tape." She managed to both sound warm and make Kadence feeling unendingly stupid all at once.

"Why didn't you just say something?" All of Kadence's anxiety, her distress, had been for nothing. Were they just watching her tear herself up for their own amusement?

"I wanted to give you the chance to tell us yourself," Gina had said, as though it were obvious. "I knew you would have told us eventually. You're a team player, Kadence."

So now here she was, flying into the white and bitter end of the world in the hopes of charming her mother's killer.

"What if I can't convince him?" Kadence had asked and Gina's smile hadn't moved, not even for a fraction of a second.

"You will," Gina said, "because you have to."

---○---

The SennTech Bot called Archie appeared at first as a dark blur upon the horizon. He had gotten ahold of an ATV somehow and had ridden it miles in from the nearest town. Ebert had seen Bots go to great lengths to find Hart, but this might take the cake.

If they were really going to stay here, though, on the furthest protruding edge of Alaska, he suspected he would see a lot more of it in the future.

It wasn't until he had driven quite close to their encampment that Ebert could see the second figure on the ATV. Another Bot? Hart had indicated that this Archie would be coming in alone.

Archie was immediately recognizable, his face bare and grinning as Ebert approached. The second person was a lump of clothing, rendered ageless and sexless by layers of winter gear and even what looked like a down comforter.

"She needs to get inside," he called to Ebert, helping the bundled figure awkwardly off the ATV. Ebert guided the two of them across the snow to the trailer and the other vehicles. Just in the couple of weeks they had been parked there, many of them had already started to look like abandoned husks, like the remnants of some distant society.

They burst into the trailer and Sylvie started, as though she had not been watching them out the window the whole time. "Sit down," Ebert said, going to fetch the small space heater they kept in the back.

Archie lowered the bundled woman on to the built-in sofa and began removing her wraps with Sylvie's assistance. "Shannon," he said, "are you okay?"

"I'm fine," came a voice from behind soggy wool. "Just really fucking cold."

In a few moments, they had stripped away the excess material to reveal a young human woman with a fluff of black hair. She looked uncomfortable but not agonized.

"Fingers and toes," Sylvie said, unlacing the girl's boots. "Show 'em."

"Really, I'm okay." She extended her hands for Sylvie, wiggling the fingers.

Sylvie examined the fingers and her toes carefully before finally grunting her approval.

"Archie was looking out for me," the girl said.

"I ran a little hot," Archie explained, "when we were coming up."

Sylvie got up out of her crouch. "That was risky," she said.

The girl on the sofa scrambled to her (bare) feet. Her face had taken on a sheen of almost manic energy. "Are you Hart?" she asked Sylvie.

"No," Sylvie snapped immediately, as though someone had asked her if she was an actual pile of shit. "I'm Sylvie. I'm a *human*." The wattage in the girl's face dimmed significantly.

"I didn't realize there were other humans here."

"It's a temporary arrangement," Sylvie told her stiffly.

"Speaking of that, though," Ebert said, solicitously placing the space heater next to Shannon's legs. "Why are you here exactly?"

"I need a mod. A brain mod." Ebert was trying

to decide how to tell her that Hart would never allow such a thing, that they had come all the way across the snow for nothing, when Shannon added, "And General Hiram Liao is my father."

———o———

Hart insisted upon examining the both of them before she agreed to anything. Without any machines or medical supplies, however, her examinations were necessarily cursory. She relied upon Shannon to tell her the truth about her full medical history. She had to believe Archie when he said that he had no kill switch and was, in this at least, independent from SennTech.

"I can do what you want," Hart pronounced finally. "But it will be crude. We don't have the facilities for a high-level mod. Right now, no one does. Do you understand what that will mean for you?"

"I was going to get this done in a motel room," Shannon said. "This can't possibly be worse."

"It can always be worse," Archie argued dourly.

Hart turned to him in surprise. "You don't want her to get the mod?" If that was the case, it made Ebert wonder why he'd bothered to bring the girl all the way up here then.

"I want her to be happy," Archie said simply. "I just wish she could be happy as she is."

Shannon shook her head. This had the feeling of an old argument. "Archie thinks this is what I am. But I don't think this has to be *all* that I am."

In the corner, Sylvie watched her with an unreadable expression.

Hart nodded. "I understand you completely. And, if this mod is what you truly want, I will do it for you." She turned to Archie, who looked as though he were biting back all his words. "I will do this mod for her, not for SennTech," Hart said. "I promise you."

Archie seemed slightly mollified by this.

"In exchange for this," Hart continued, "I would like you to tell me a little bit more about

SennTech, Archie. For example, would you trust them?"

Archie considered this for a long moment. "That would depend," he pronounced finally, "on what you were trusting them to do."

—o—

Kadence could not stifle it, that little flicker of geeky thrill at the prospect of actually meeting the very first Hart Series. It was not something she had ever expected and it felt, even under these monstrous circumstances, like an honor.

Gina was clearly struck as well. "My goodness," she said, shaking Hart's hand vigorously, "you're just perfect, aren't you?" Kadence found herself thinking that she was going to have a hard time getting her Bots approved at SennTech now that Gina had seen what was theoretically possible with the form. Then she remembered that, if they made it out of this somehow, she was going to run as far and as fast away from SennTech as she could manage.

"Hi," Kadence muttered when it was her turn. Even in the Alaskan winter, Hart's hand was warm.

Kadence had never done anything like this. A . . . parlay? A détente? She didn't know exactly what the protocol was but she was still surprised when Hart led them into a large mobile trailer where a number of people were gathered. The group included Shannon Liao, who looked younger in person somehow and, of course, Archie.

Kadence had been preparing herself the entire trip for this moment. She had practiced a number of conversation openers from the outraged to the tearful to the flippant. Here, though, with him looking at her and smiling that dopey smile, she found that she could not say anything at all.

He waved weakly.

It was the wave that, somehow, made her want to reach out and slap him. The violence of the urge surprised her and so Kadence sat down on the long sofa next to a good-looking man with longish black hair.

"Hi," he said quietly as she sank into the cushions. "I'm Ebert."

"Kadence," she murmured.

"It seems silly to come all this way for a short conversation," Gina said, smiling, "but I'm afraid I don't have a lot to say. SennTech's position is simple: we love Bots. Bots are our livelihood. We are natural allies here! We cannot survive without Bots and, increasingly, it's looking like you cannot survive without us. SennTech has political clout and money. A lot of money. We can negotiate with the US military. But we need your cooperation. And a little bit of leverage."

She stared straight across the room at Shannon Liao, who looked supremely skeptical in return.

Hart nodded gently, as though she were digesting Gina's words. "You're slavers," she said eventually, "and pimps."

Gina looked slightly taken aback. "We fill a need—"

"You produce sex slaves and other indentured servants. You specialize in children."

Gina paused to gather herself. She closed her eyes as though instructions might have been written on the lid. "We do," she said. "But we are not attempting to destroy you. It is not and never will be in our best interests to destroy Bots. We can accept that there will be communities of non-SennTech Bots and we can certainly agree that we would not interfere in the management of such communities. Who else will give you that kind of guarantee?"

"We want a retirement program. If a SennTech Bot's original purchaser dies or abdicates responsibility for the Bot, you must give them the option to leave the industry."

Gina smiled. This was a negotiation. This, she knew how to do.

"I think we could make that work," she said.

"And we want Kadence DeSouza to be our liaison."

On the sofa, Kadence's head shot up. "What? Me?" she asked.

"I have been told that you . . . have a soul,"
Hart told her.

Kadence knew of course that there were only a
handful of people in the world who would have
told her that. One of them was standing in this
room right now. She looked at Archie, only to find
his eyes shining with encouragement.

"Kadence is a brilliant roboticist," Gina said,
"but she's not really—"

"I've told you our conditions. Yes or no."

"We can't just elevate—"

Kadence found herself suddenly on her feet. "I'll
do it," she said.

Gina made a little abortive noise of protest but
Hart ignored her utterly. Instead, she stretched her
hand out to Kadence once again. "We have a deal,
then," Hart said. She had such a beautiful smile.
What marvels humans made.

———o———

"It's a shame," Sylvie said, passing the razor close to the curve of the young woman's skull. "You have beautiful hair."

"Hair grows back," Shannon said easily.

"You aren't . . . afraid at all?" Sylvie asked as a dark curl of hair tumbled to the floor.

"Nah, I've gotten lots of haircuts before."

"I meant the mod."

Shannon nodded and sent the razor bumping erratically to one side. "Sorry," she muttered sheepishly.

"It's all coming off anyway."

"But to answer your question, no. I'm not afraid."

Sylvie gave a heavy sigh. "Well. You're a brave girl, then."

"You're the brave one, following the Bots all the way up here."

Sylvie frowned. "It wasn't exactly by choice."

By now, she had shorn off roughly half of Shannon's hair, making her look like a lunatic on the run from the asylum. Perhaps, Sylvie thought, that wasn't so far off from the truth.

"What happened?"

Sylvie hesitated. Like everyone else, she knew who Shannon's father was and what that meant. The girl probably had an idea of her father and his work. It might be . . . distressing to hear anything that contradicted that idea.

But Shannon was an adult. Wasn't that what she was trying to tell everyone with this fool's errand to get her brain sliced up?

"We were attacked," Sylvie said, "by a group of soldiers. They killed several of us and I believe they would have killed all of us if the Bot woman had not come."

Shannon's silence seemed weighty but Sylvie could not tell exactly what the girl might be thinking. The razor went *buzz, buzz, buzz.*

"Do you know what happens to the recalled Bots?" Shannon asked finally in an impossibly small voice. "No one else can tell me. Or they won't tell me."

"All I've heard are rumors," Sylvie admitted. No one, after all, had survived the recall process to tell about it. "But . . . they say they burn them in an incredibly hot furnace. That's the only way to really destroy those things."

Shannon trembled under the razor. "That's horrible," she said.

"I suppose so."

Shannon half turned to look at her and Sylvie *tsked* as the razor mowed through her hair at a bizarre angle. "You *suppose so*? You live amongst them. Can't you imagine what that's like? Can't you imagine what it's like for someone who—" Shannon choked slightly—"loves a Bot?"

The razor was still buzzing but Sylvie was still holding it in place uselessly. Could she understand what it was to feel for a Bot? To even . . .

Perhaps.

Perhaps she could.

"Let's get you finished," Sylvie said, tilting Shannon's chin back with her hand. "We don't have much time."

ELEVEN
FORGED

Isla Redonda, Mexico. November, 2047.

"**N**eutral territory," they had said, but Isla Redondo was perhaps the least neutral territory that General Liao could have imagined. He didn't really care, though, exactly where the Bots wanted to meet so long as he could seed his people all around the location, ready to take the original Hart Series into custody. That would be important, symbolically. To destroy the first and most prominent of them would deal a huge blow to the little straggling resistance.

As he waited, though, on that island where everything had once been made clear to him, he felt a gnawing sense of worry. This meeting made no sense from the Bots perspective. He had made his position very clear to them and if they thought he was interested in a negotiation, they were deluded.

They must truly believe, Hiram thought, that they had something that he wanted.

"Maybe they're desperate?" Janelle had suggested. "It could be a last-ditch effort."

It was a reasonable conclusion for her to make, but Janelle was a scientist, not really a soldier. Liao had been dealing in the business of war nearly all of his adult life and, in his experience, enemies simply didn't behave this way.

He was not afraid of being overpowered, however. They had been starving the Bots of parts and materials for years. Sinking the Woodrow Wilson had cost them thousands of bodies. They were wounded and running with no hope of incoming supplies. Hiram felt confident that he had the upper hand and, if he didn't, he was fully prepared to launch a full aerial strike against the island, and then they could all burn together.

As he waited for the Bot boat to arrive, Hiram wandered around the island. He was realizing just now that, despite the large space this island occupied in his consciousness, he had never actually set foot on Isla Redondo before.

He'd even found the place at the top of the island, the old bunker where they had been living. It looked like any other abandoned industrial site. It looked like nothing of importance had ever happened there.

It was fitting, though, that the bunker was the place where Hart and her people found him.

Generally speaking, Bots did not age. At least the HS units that had been produced under his command did not age; he had no idea what sort of strange maladies Edmond West might have deemed vital for his precious Hart. Liao wondered about this because, though it had been less than five years since he had seen her, the Hart Bot looked visibly older. Where there was once something indelibly girlish about her there was now a . . . heaviness to all of her movements.

He could only imagine what he looked like to her.

She was alone. That was surprising. Surely she could not be so foolhardy as to come without any support at all?

"I know you're eager to begin," she said, smiling at him. Smiling, of all things. "But, first, I want to show you something."

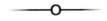

He should have called in the team up at the bunker. He should have commanded them to swarm the island, capturing Hart whatever it took. Instead, he had allowed curiosity to lead him down and down through the green trees and on to the sand where so many Bots had met their end.

A boat was docked there. In front of it stood a man that Liao didn't immediately recognize as well as the bureaucratic little grasper from SennTech.

Ever since the raid, he had been fielding constant legal volleys from the company. They were apparently under the mistaken impression that the threat of a lawsuit in any way scared him.

"She can come out now," Hart called to someone he couldn't see, who was still inside the ship.

They—there were two of them—emerged slowly and, ridiculously enough, it was the man that Liao recognized first. The Archie boy that his daughter had brought to the house. He was helping a slightly hunched figure, who was moving slowly.

When Liao realized that figure was, in fact, his Shannon, the first thing he thought of was Nora. Nora, in the last months of her life when her long hair, which he had spent years cleaning out of drains and shaking out of sheets, grew brittle and thin from the medication. She might have kept her mane, but she decided instead to buzz it off. "It'll be easier," she had told him. She had never had short hair in her life and she talked the whole time about how light it would feel, how free. But Hiram remembered the awful, stricken look on her face when she had finally looked in the mirror.

Shannon looked even worse. Her skull bulged noticeably just above her left ear and there was a vivid pink scar visible to Hiram even from the beach. She was moving slowly and her face was set as though each step required all of her concentration.

He moved to her without thinking. "Shannon," he said, pulling her away from Archie's grip. The boy look for a second as though he wanted to resist but Hart shook her head at him.

Hiram held his daughter by her shoulders and searched her face. "Shannon," he said again. It felt almost as though he were declaring her, giving her a name just as he had done when she was born.

"'Hi, Dad," she said softly.

"Are you in pain?"

She shook her head barely an inch in either direction. "I'm still healing," she admitted. "But it's not too bad. No worse than when I had to get knee surgery in high school."

"Shannon, what have you done?" He meant it to sound angry—he was angry—but somehow it emerged from him as a sigh.

"I fixed something that was wrong."

Up close, the scars on her head were shiny with lymph fluid. Oh, his girl. His poor girl. How had this become her only solution? Hiram Liao knew that he had not been a perfect father, but he had always looked at his Shannon, successful, happy, healthy, well-adjusted and believed that, whatever his flaws, he could not have done too badly. Here was evidence that he could not deny, however, of just how deeply he had failed her.

"Your daughter is now as much a Bot as Christopher Fogel," the SennTech woman said. Her face looked like it was twitching to twist into the smile. "And she's not the only one. The world is full of people like Shannon who need Bot mods. And people like you, who love them. Destroying them all won't be easy. Especially since you'd probably have to start with her," she jerked her thumb at Shannon.

"Or else it starts to look kind of hypocritical." She was truly smiling now. Hiram wanted to wipe it off her face, preferably in a smear of blood.

That rage did not mean that she was wrong, however. In fact, Hiram suspected that it meant just the opposite. Somehow, the world had fundamentally shifted in the time it took him to walk down to the beach. Just a few minutes ago, he had been ready to shower them all in fire, now . . . Now, he could not seem to look away from his wounded daughter, her new scars and the hesitancy of her steps. She had deserved better, from life and from him.

"What do you want?" he asked them through gritted teeth.

———○———

"What the fuck is a Feltian Plateau?"

"It's a micro-continent," Hart said. "Or it was about eighty million years ago. Right now, it's underneath the Beaufort Sea off the coast of Alaska."

"You want . . . water rights?" Liao was struggling to understand. She smiled at him indulgently, as though he might be forgiven his dullness. Liao was not sure who he hated more: her or the SennTech woman.

"No. I want the land when it rises."

"When it *rises*?"

"It should be within the next six years, if my calculations are correct." *And my calculations are always correct*, she did not bother to add, but he could read it clearly on her smug face. "I intend to establish a Bot nation there, a sovereign nation in every respect. I want the United States to acknowledge it as such."

On one hand, what was it to him, giving away a land mass that did not—and might never—exist? On the other hand a country full of Bots was a nightmare scenario.

"What assurances do I have that this . . . Bot

nation won't immediately make war on humanity and obliterate us?"

"None," Hart admitted. "I will also demand your trust, which should have been ours from the beginning. You made us, you owe us the opportunity to become our fullest selves."

"If," Liao began slowly, "I were to entertain something like this, there would have to be certain safeguards in place. You ask to be a true nation of the world and you also ask for the trust of the United States, you must know by now how impossible that is?

All Bots would need to be identified, registered and licensed with some sort of obvious external marking—no more of this behind the ear bullshit—that makes their nature plain. And we would have to agree to a cap on the number of Bots the both of you could produce in a year. Both the Bot nation and SennTech would need to submit to regular inspections to make sure that these specifications were behind adhered to."

The SennTech woman looked faintly offended but Hart just gave him a steady nod.

"That is agreeable," she said.

"We are also going to need something else. Something symbolic." Hiram began thinking now of how he would return to the military and explain this turn of events. How could he tell them that his apocalyptic warnings had been wrong?

They weren't, of course. But Hiram Liao had discovered just today that there were limits to even his ability to sacrifice for the greater good.

"We cannot hand the leadership of a potentially hostile nation over to someone with such a brutal history," Hiram said. The other man, whose name Liao had never actually gotten, looked to Hart, bewildered. Hart, however, seemed to understand exactly what Hiram was saying.

"I understand," she said. "What I did was wrong and I will submit to human justice, as it was the humans that I have wronged."

"A human who murdered nine servicemen in an un-provoked attack would be executed."

The other man had caught on now.

"No!" he said, "that's absurd. It wasn't *unprovoked* and how many Bots have you destroyed—"

Hart interrupted him with a look. "Ebert," she said gently, "don't. If I cannot face the consequences of my actions now, our new country will have no integrity at all. I don't want us to remain a runaway nation forever, do you?"

"There are other ways to do this," the man insisted, "but we can't continue without you."

Hart laughed lightly. "Of course you can. In fact, it's probably for the best. The Bot nation is more than one person. More than me. And this will prove it."

The man looked like he wanted to say more but Hart gave his hand a squeeze. "Ebert, I need you and Sylvie to look after them, all of our people. Can you do that for me?"

"Of course. But—"

"Then it's decided," Hart said briskly, turning back to Hiram. "We are in agreement." She paused and Liao could not understand the look on her face. It looked strangely—even supremely—satisfied. "Doesn't that feel better? To be together again?" she murmured but Liao got the impression that she wasn't talking to any of them at all.

---O---

After Alaska, after Isla Redondo, when Kadence returned to her little apartment, she laid down on her sofa and slept in her clothes. She didn't wake up for twenty-two hours. When she awoke, her flex-tablet was alive with calls and messages and it was Monday morning.

She went to the SennTech offices on a kind of autopilot. The offices felt almost abandoned with only a scanty handful of human employees here and there. Never a particularly loud environment, it now felt like walking into a place where the silence was heavy and holy, like a cemetery crypt.

When she arrived at her lab she began the process of separating her own materials from those provided by SennTech. It was easier than she'd thought; there was very little here that belonged to her.

Gina surprised her with an actual knock. She even waited for Kadence to nod before barging in. "Okay, so I've been working all week with some of our concept people reporting my observations of the original Hart Series and I think we've come up with some very interesting innovations . . . " she trailed off, noticing Kadence's messenger bag, a coffee mug, a few paper documents and an alternate pair of shoes sticking out of the top. "What are you doing?" Gina asked.

"Packing my shit," Kadence said, not looking up at her. "In the broader sense, getting out of here."

"But you agreed—"

"I agreed to be a liaison for the Bots. That's all. Not a roboticist, not a developer, not even a lab tech. So, if the Bots want to talk to me, then you give me a call but, other than that, I don't ever want to see the inside of this place again."

"Kadence . . . " She hated it when Gina got that disappointed tone in her voice. Who did Gina think she was, Kadence's mother?

Over the years, Kadence had frequently fantasized about how she might quit SennTech, the invectives she might spit, the crushing put-downs, the righteous moral fury. Now, though, that the actual moment had come, she found herself saying simply, "Gina, SennTech has made everything worse."

Gina shook her head and reached out to grab Kadence's hand. Kadence was too slow to pull away and she could not escape from Gina's shockingly strong grip. "I know. Trust me, I know better than anyone. But, Kadence, what if I could promise you that all the suffering and all the cruelty, all of that was in service to something so much greater?"

"What are you talking about?"

"I know what you think of us. Heartless and soulless and all about money but that's not the whole story, Kadence. SennTech does have a goal, it has a vision. SennTech is going to transform the world."

This didn't clarify anything for Kadence but she did see something in Gina's face that she had never encountered there before: sincerity.

"Come on," Gina smiled, like they were old friends. Maybe they were, by now. "I know that you can produce the level of Bot we saw in Alaska. In fact, I think you're the *only* person who can. Come with us. Come save the world with us."

Kadence looked at her face, at their joined hands, at her half-packed bag. She extracted one hand from Gina's grip with considerable difficulty and reached into the back, pulling out the coffee cup and sitting it on her work desk. "Okay," she said, "but I want a hell of a raise."

——o——

"I don't understand any of this. Does it make more sense to . . . a Bot?" Sylvie perched uncertainly in the chair that Hart had often occupied before the cobbled-together computer monitors.

"Not this Bot," Ebert said, scrolling through the endless columns of data. "From what I can tell, Hart discovered that the Pacific Desalination Project had been . . . disrupting? I guess? The various sea levels. She seemed to think that, if certain things fell into place, including what looks like a pretty big explosion . . . the land mass would rise from the ocean. Or rather, the waters would recede to expose it."

"That sounds insane," Sylvie said, matter-of-factly. She was right, it did sound insane. It was the kind of thing that only Hart could have gotten the Bots to pursue.

"You're going to have to think of a much better way to pitch it when you tell the others," Sylvie continued. Ebert gave her a startled look.

"You think . . . I mean . . . I don't think they're going to listen to me."

"Not if you bring that shitty energy to it. Hart put you in charge for a reason."

Ebert laughed, but it was joyless, the kind of sound one made when all other reactions were exhausted. "I don't know why Hart did anything."

Sylvie turned in her chair until she was facing him. "I do," she said. She held his gaze, her eyes were big and brown and he wanted to look away but he also never wanted to look at anything else ever again. "You're a good leader, Ebert. You think about your people before yourself and you have mettle. Hart wasn't crazy and she wasn't stupid, so I think this sinking water land thing is going to work and I think you are the right person to make it happen."

"She didn't just put me in charge, you know. I could use a partner." Ebert pointed out.

There was a flicker on Sylvie's face, the indecision that she kept buried deep in her gut. It fluttered away only to be replaced by her customary resolve. "Of course," she said simply. "They need us."

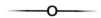

Hart, who had left the military lab like a bullet from a gun, returned eminently subdued. They did not even bother to cuff her. Not that cuffs existed that could contain a Bot of Hart's caliber.

Her request—her only request—was that she be allowed to look in on the lab before she ventured to the furnace. Hiram and Janelle stood by the door stiffly while she walked around the room, touching each surface like someone wandering in a dream, trying to determine what was real.

"I was born here," she marveled once, under her breath.

When she had made a full circuit of the room, she turned back to the two of them. "It hasn't changed," she said. Janelle nodded. Hiram, who did not know how to respond to that, said nothing.

Hart allowed herself then to be escorted to the furnace. Normally, they had to drop Bots through from the floor above and let gravity do the work of subduing the units.

Hart preferred to walk.

By the time Hiram and Janelle had retreated to the observation room, Hart had entered the furnace room. They saw her face contort as she hit that first wall of heat. Still, she continued onward in a series of regular, deliberate steps.

"Oh God," Janelle said, "we shouldn't have done any of this."

"There won't be anything left," Hiram said. "It will be like it never happened."

They both knew that was a lie, so there was

no need to say so. Janelle took his hand and there was nothing warm or affectionate in the gesture. Instead, it was the clinging grip of a drowning swimmer.

Hart approached the open maw of the furnace proper. Her face has started to look . . . wrong as the PolyX compound she was made of began to melt. She looked curiously into the flames until her eyes transformed, tarnished into a watery white. The heat had blinded her and so she reached out with her hands, feeling with dripping fingertips the lip of the furnace and raising her leg slowly to crawl inside.

It took less than two minutes, all things considered.

Afterwards, there was just a pile of ash and they had burned so many hundreds of Bots that who could say which gray, anonymous particles used to be Hart? The first truly human robot was as gone as they could make her and this small piece, at least, of humanity's grave mistake had been rectified.

EPILOGUE

SAN FRANCISCO, CA. DECEMBER, 2047.

"The hair will grow back," Hiram told his daughter, because that seemed like the sort of thing that she might care about.

She didn't, though. "I know," she said, brushing her hand over the dark bristle of hair that was already coming in.

Perhaps, by the time he saw her again, her hair would be long and glossy once more.

"Do you . . . feel different?"

Shannon shrugged. "I don't feel afraid all the time. I don't feel ashamed. I don't feel weak."

Hiram wanted to say that he was sorry, though he could not pinpoint what, exactly, he was sorry for. He thought that she would find an incomplete apology more galling than none at all, so he said nothing.

"Wait here," Hiram said, a sudden inspiration striking him, "there's something I'd like to give you."

In the study, he rifled through his travel bag and found in the front pocket, just as he had expected, an intricate knot on a string. It was small and old, stiff from being tucked in that pocket for who knew how many years. Nevertheless, it felt good to have something tangible to offer to his daughter. His only child.

"Here," he said, dropping the knot into Shannon's hand.

"Is this a . . . rope? A knotted rope?" she asked, turning it over in her palm. Of course she would be bewildered; Hiram had never evinced any particular attachment to any Chinese art forms before.

"Nǎinai gave that to me to take when I travel. It's good," he said awkwardly, "for trips. For journeys."

Shannon closed her fist around the knot and looked up at him. "Thank you," she said, smiling her first genuine smile.

———o———

"How did it go?" Archie asked as Shannon slid into the passenger seat.

"Better than I expected," Shannon admitted, tucking the little knot into the pocket of her jeans.

Archie smiled at her. "I'm glad."

Shannon smiled back before tipping down the visor and checking her scar in the mirror. She wanted to make sure it healed cleanly. It looked okay, but she drew her fingertip lightly down its surface to feel how raised it was.

The action stirred in her something. A kind of . . . memory or something. The Bots in Alaska had told her that something like that might happen. Side effects of re-wiring her brains using synthetic materials from a donor. This was the first time, however, that she'd actually felt like something . . . *other* was sharing her head.

When she touched the scar, it felt to her incorrect. She had a sense—something more than visual—of another scar, this one on her lower abdomen right over her uterus. She had a sense of the way it felt underneath her own fingers, and she knew what it felt like when someone else—a man, she felt sure—touched it. It had been secret and important. It made her feel powerful.

"Are you okay?" Archie asked her and Shannon realized she had been staring uselessly into the visor mirror for nearly a minute.

"Yeah," she said, turning to him and grinning. "I'm wonderful."